THEIR BRIDE

THEIRS
BOOK FOUR

JESS MICHAELS

For You. Wherever the road leads, it's been an amazing ride.

For Michael, the best day of my life is any day with you. Thank you for always being next to me for the highs and lows.

PROLOGUE

Summer 1811
Benedict

"Christ, he weighs twice as much when he's drunk," Benedict Norfolk laughed as he adjusted the weight of his friend, Viscount Arthur Warwick, against his shoulder.

Warwick's younger brother, Darrius, grunted with equal strain from the other side of the viscount. "He might be doing it on purpose."

"I'm not doing itsh on porpoise," Arthur said, looking over at Benedict and breathing rancid breath in his face.

They stumbled up the stairs together, laughing awkwardly, bumping the banister and the walls respectively as Arthur grumbled out drunken nonsense. Finally they reached the door to his chamber and Darrius flopped the lion's share of Arthur's weight onto Benedict so he could open the door.

"Give him here," Darrius said, meeting Benedict's eyes for a moment before he darted them away.

Benedict sighed. These two men were his best friends. He'd tell the world that if anyone asked, as would they, he knew. But he and

Darrius…well, that was complicated. Far too complicated for Darrius's taste, clearly.

"Why do you want to help all of a shudden?" Arthur asked, glaring at his brother while the two men led him to his bed. "You're the younger one, you know. I'm the vishcunt."

Benedict snorted. "You are that. Flop him down on the bed and I'll get his boots."

Darrius did so, sprawling Arthur on his stomach with his head somewhat off the edge of the bed, probably to keep him from choking on vomit if he cast up his accounts in the night. Benedict tugged on his friend's boots, but the drink he'd had, himself, wasn't exactly keeping his head from spinning. He stumbled a little and Darrius reached out, catching his arm, drawing him a bit closer to steady him.

They stood like that for a moment, faces too close together in the dim firelight of Arthur's room. Above the throbbing of his heart, Benedict heard Darrius's breath hitch. Then Darrius released him and pivoted back to his brother.

He grabbed Arthur's foot and gave a great tug, removing the boot in one smooth motion. He repeated the action on the other side and tossed the boots away. Already Arthur was snoring, passed out. All but dead to the world.

Darrius made a soft noise of discontent and strode from the chamber without another word for Benedict. Benedict followed, shutting the door softly behind himself. Darrius had stopped in the hallway and turned to face Benedict.

His expression was unreadable, but then again, that handsome face was almost always that way. Well, that wasn't entirely true. One was never uncertain when Darrius Warwick was angry. His brows dropped and a wrinkle formed between them, his full lips tightened and his jaw flexed.

But he wasn't doing that now. No, he looked entirely blank. "We should have stopped after the second club. I knew he was too deep in his cups."

Benedict tilted his head. "He keeps control until he loses control. He's always been that way." He shifted a step closer. "You too."

Darrius glared at him. "I don't lose control."

A laugh was the only response Benedict could come up with, though he found this situation not funny in the slightest. "Of course not."

Darrius's nostrils flared and now he *was* starting to look angry. "What the bloody hell does that mean?"

Benedict drew a short breath. He and Darrius had been dancing around this conversation for years. Avoiding it. Playing it off. Creating distance between themselves so they would never have to have it.

Would he be brave enough to broach the topic now, standing in this hallway in the middle of the night, tipsy enough to have some inhibitions removed, sober enough to know what might happen next could have consequences?

No. He wasn't.

"Nothing," he grunted. "It's always nothing, isn't it?"

Darrius's breath was short as his gaze flitted down the entire length of Benedict's body and made him want. Want. Always want. Want things he couldn't have, at least not with this man. Sometimes with other men. He knew what he was. What he desired. Sometimes ladies, sometimes gentlemen, sometimes both.

But Darrius squashed any part of himself that wasn't in control. He'd never let this go so far.

"What do you want from me?" he asked.

Benedict blinked. There was something almost plaintive in that question. As if his friend, his best friend, his most cherished friend and companion…needed him to be the one to lead. For once.

"The same thing you want from me," Benedict dared to whisper, moving another step closer. Now he could feel Darrius's body heat. "The same thing we've both wanted for years and pretended didn't exist. I want that, Darrius."

Darrius stared at Benedict, his mouth opening and shutting.

Then he pivoted away and stomped down the hall toward the chamber he'd grown up in. He wasn't returning to his home across Town, it seemed.

"I don't know what you're talking about," he tossed back over his shoulder.

Benedict stung from the rejection. And he had drunk just enough to feel another emotion he rarely allowed when it came to this subject: anger. Darrius asked him the question then pretended not to understand the answer? It was so bloody unfair.

He followed after him, passing through the door into Darrius's chamber right at his heels. "Lie to yourself, but stop lying to me," Benedict snapped. "And stop teasing if you aren't going to play."

"What does that mean?" Darrius asked.

Benedict reached back and slammed the door behind himself. This was not a conversation to have where prying ears might hear, even if the servants were already abed. "You know what it means."

Darrius stood there, his hands gripped so tightly at his sides that his knuckles were white. Then he looked down the length of Benedict for the second time. Knowing it was likely the best invitation he'd get, Benedict closed the remaining distance between them. He reached out, resting a hand on Darrius's shoulder as he stared into his remarkable, captivating blue eyes. Jesus, those eyes.

"You don't have to pretend this away," he whispered, and leaned closer, so his lips almost touched Darrius's. Oh, how he wanted this. Just as he had for a good portion of his life. And being this close...it was the most beautiful torture.

But just as he was about to kiss Darrius, the other man pressed hand to his chest and shoved him back. Back farther, three long steps until Benedict hit the door. Darrius's face was still close to his and his eyes were lit with so many tangled emotions. So many uncertainties and questions.

He didn't kiss Benedict, even though Darrius tilted his head and let his breath sweep over his lips. Instead he shocked Benedict to his very core by dropping to his knees before him.

"Darrius," he whispered.

"Shut up," Darrius responded, and with a flick of his wrist, he unfastened the fall front on Benedict's trousers. It fell forward and his cock was revealed.

He was already starting to get hard just from seeing Darrius on his knees before him, but when Darrius caught him in hand, looking up at him as he stroked his length, full hardness was instantaneous and almost painfully sensitive. He surged forward, almost against his will and Darrius let out a groan as if this pleased him as much.

Darrius's grip tightened as he leaned forward, brushing the head of Benedict's cock against his cheek, letting him feel the rough beginnings of stubble on the sensitive flesh.

"Please," Benedict choked out, helpless as he gripped his fingers against the door.

Darrius said nothing, he just turned his face, and his mouth closed around Benedict, taking his full length deep into his throat. Benedict almost lost consciousness with the sensation of wet heat, gentle suction, the swirl of Darrius's tongue against his length, *around* his length.

"Fuck," he breathed, dropping his head back to thunk against the door and dragging a hand into Darrius's thick hair. As the locks tangled around his fingers, Darrius let out a moan that vibrated against Benedict's cock, streaking pleasure through what felt like every nerve in his body.

He began to take Benedict deeper, harder, faster, sucking and licking. They moaned in time together as Benedict thrust, pleasure driving him out of control, the buzz of liquor keeping him from overthinking anything but sensation. He just wanted to take this man's mouth, he wanted to come, he wanted to make Darrius come afterward until they were a sweaty pile of satiated pleasure.

Then he wanted to sleep and start all over again in the morning.

Those thoughts and all others fled his mind as Darrius began slower, deeper, more purposeful tugs on his cock with his mouth. He stroked the base with his hand, too, drawing out his release from him with purpose and drive. Benedict couldn't resist him, even if he wanted to, which he didn't. He shut his eyes, he let the waves rush over him and he came.

Darrius didn't stop mouth-fucking him, taking every drop of his release without hesitation until he sagged against the door, panting and weak with pleasure. He opened his eyes and looked down at Darrius, still on his knees, hair mussed from Benedict's fingers, gaze bright with passion.

And then something shifted. The light went out of those blue eyes, replaced with recognition and worse, regret.

"There, now you've had what you want," Darrius grunted, wiping the remnants of slick pleasure from his shining lips as he pushed to his feet.

Benedict reached for him. Now was not the time to hold back anymore. Now that he had felt this man's passion, he had to try harder. "That *isn't* all I want, Darrius."

There was a moment when Darrius froze, staring at him almost as if he didn't understand those words. Or perhaps he understood them far too well.

"Well, it's all we'll ever have," Darrius said, stepping away from him, turning his back. "And it will *never* be repeated."

Benedict stared at him. Heard the finality in his voice. Saw it in the way he straightened his shoulders and refused to turn back. And Benedict's heart broke in his chest, that feeling of grief replacing all the pleasure he'd just felt with this man. He knew Darrius too well. If he declared a position, it was almost impossible to change it. He was stone, too hard to be permeated, even by hope.

"I'm sorry you feel that way," he choked out. He wanted to say a thousand other things, imprudent things, true things. But he couldn't. Not now. Not ever. So he turned on his heel and left the chamber, tucking himself back into place as he did.

And hating that this is what they'd come to, hating what it would do to them from this moment forward.

CHAPTER 1

Two Years Later
Vanessa

Miss Vanessa Gardner looked in the mirror and hardly recognized the vision she saw. It was her face that looked back at her, of course, though with paler cheeks than normal. But it didn't seem like her body, cloaked in the finest gown she'd ever worn. Her wedding gown, with a light yellow pelisse that had elbow-length sleeves with crisscrossed lace accents. Beneath was a white gown, with a finely brocaded skirt. Her dark hair was piled high on her head, interwound with jewels and flowers from the garden right here in Brightvale, her intended's estate in the seat of Warwick.

Her intended. That part didn't seem right, either. It had happened too fast, been too rushed. And it hadn't been her choice. Her parents had seen an opportunity to undo damage done two years ago and they had taken it with barely a by your leave to her.

Such was her life. She was a commodity to be traded, for good or for ill. Like a horse or a goose or a plot of unentailed land. Something to be handed off along with their piles of money in exchange for connection to a title, something that would elevate their status in Society. In this case, the Viscount of Warwick.

Arthur.

Sometimes Vanessa forgot his name, truth be told. She'd stare at him across a room and for a moment her mind would go blank. And then she'd find it again, to her great relief, and try to find some way to permanently attach it to her mind. But perhaps after today it would stick. Or after tonight when they had made the union legal in body, as well as by law.

She shivered. She wasn't really looking forward to that, either. The viscount never looked at her with desire. She didn't feel any for him.

"What a marriage," she whispered, and bent her head. Then she pushed the thoughts away. Save jumping out the window and running away, there was no escape. She found herself leaning closer and looking out said window. No, she was too high up to survive the fall. So matrimony it was and there was no avoiding it.

She sighed and looked toward the door. It was odd that she was still alone. Unlike most days, her maid, Mary, had not been the one to ready her this morning. Taken ill, the woman who had done the work in her place had said. Strange since Mary had seemed fine the night before when she helped Vanessa in her nightly preparations. Distant, perhaps, but not unwell.

And Vanessa's mother hadn't joined her either, nor her father, as she readied herself. She had a few friends who had made the trip to Warwick for the ceremony, but the most important of that small number had also not been seen yet, either. Had she been abandoned? Or perhaps the world had come to an end and she was the last woman standing.

With a little smile at the ridiculousness of that notion, she moved to the door and opened it, looking out into the quiet hallway. For a house about to host a wedding, there was no pageantry or celebration to be heard.

"It's more like a wake," she muttered, and crept down the hallway toward the stairs. Still there was only silence to greet her, and so she decided to go down and began peeking into parlors for anyone who could help her pass the time until she was marched down the aisle to her fate.

Her future. She had meant her future, of course. Fate sounded so dire.

"Miss Gardner."

She froze at the sound of her name being spoken behind her. She recognized the voice, even though she had heard it used very rarely. Slowly she turned and found herself face to face with Warwick's friend, Mr. Benedict Norfolk. God help her, but she caught her breath at the sight of him wearing his formal clothing. He was, after all, one of those meant to stand up with her intended and witness their walk into a lifetime together.

He was devastatingly handsome, this man. Tall and lanky, with a wiry strength about him that his casual swagger said he didn't feel driven to prove. He had an angled face with high cheekbones and brown eyes that were always bright. Like he'd been laughing just before he saw you. And he always had a smile on his face.

Except for now. Now he was just staring at her, his mouth a little slack. He cleared his throat and said again, "Miss Gardner. You are lovely."

Heat filled her cheeks and moved decidedly southward down her betrayer of a body. Her future husband she felt nothing for. This man...well, she wouldn't consider it.

She bent her head so that he could no longer hold her gaze. "Thank you, Mr. Norfolk."

"I'm surprised to see you roaming the halls—I thought you were meant to be secreted away until the big reveal as you were led down the aisle."

"Yes," she said with a shake of her head. "And yet I've seen no one this morning beyond one of the household maids. I was contemplating whether I was the last one left on earth, actually. But here you are."

He chuckled and the low sound worked up her spine. "Perhaps we are the last two. I suppose it would fall on us to repop—" He cut himself off with a shake of his head. "That's a distasteful joke, I apologize."

She found her breath short. She wasn't offended by the words she knew he was about to say. But she didn't find them funny, considering she'd been contemplating her attraction to the man. If they were the last two left, she could have done far worse for a companion.

"I don't suppose you've seen my father or mother?" she asked, choosing not to address the matter.

His brow wrinkled a little. "No. You know, now that you say it, I realize I haven't seen much of anyone this morning either. Why don't you allow me to escort you downstairs? We can search them out together."

He held out an arm as he said it and she stared at it. It was a very nice arm, she could see that even when it was encased in layers of fabric. There was no way to deny him, so she slid a hand into the crook of his elbow and tried not to suck in a little breath of awareness. He smiled at her, then led her down the stairs.

Together they moved along the hallway, looking in parlors and other chambers for any of the wedding guests or family members. At last she opened a door and inside was one of her dearest friends, the Marchioness of Egerton. Relief swelled in her when she saw Merritt, and she released Mr. Norfolk as she stepped inside.

Merritt rose and drew in a long breath. "Oh, Vanessa! You are gorgeous!"

"Thank you, as are you," Vanessa said as they exchanged a kiss on each cheek.

Merritt looked past her toward Mr. Norfolk, and then she gave Vanessa questioning stare that made her blush. "Mr...Norfolk, isn't it?" she said. "Good morning."

He inclined his head even as his gaze slid to Vanessa again. "Lady Egerton."

"Mr. Norfolk found me searching for my family and was kind enough to escort me downstairs. Have you seen my mother or father, Merritt?"

Merritt let out a sigh. "Not your father, though your mother was with me for a short time. She seemed extremely anxious about something but would not share the details. She just kept pacing and looking at the door."

Vanessa swallowed. Of course, her mother was probably just anticipating the wedding. She was desperate to see her daughter wed and receive whatever benefits she hoped to get from the marriage. And yet Vanessa had a strange sense of foreboding now.

She looked at Norfolk and found he was also frowning, though he erased the expression from his face and replaced it with a shadow version of his usual smile. "Forgive me, ladies, I shall leave you two and see if I can find the groom and his brother."

She worried her hands before her, wishing he wouldn't go in that moment when she felt a little uncertain. But she shook the inappropriate desire away and forced her own smile. "Of course. Thank you again."

He bowed slightly to them both and then left the room. When he was gone, Merritt caught her hands and guided her to the settee. "He is very handsome, isn't he?"

Vanessa gave her a little glare. "Gracious, it's my wedding day."

A laugh was Merritt's response. "It doesn't change facts. But perhaps you think Darrius Warwick the more handsome one."

"Alvin is who I'm marrying," Vanessa said through clenched teeth. Merritt's eyes went wide and Vanessa realized what she'd done. "Arthur!" she corrected swiftly. "I meant *Arthur*. And I never should have told you that I found his brother handsome."

Now Merritt's expression fell a little. "Firstly, you cannot shock me, as you know. So you are more than allowed to confess such secrets without fear of judgment. And secondly, Vanessa…is this marriage what you want?"

Vanessa bent her head. "Do not ask me that. It is happening, I must resign myself. Look at you, you were wed in an arrangement not so different and you are very happy with the marquess now."

"I could recall Elliot's name on my wedding day," Merritt said softly.

Vanessa pursed her lips. "I can't escape it. There is no point in working myself into a frenzy about it."

"I could help you," Merritt said.

Vanessa understood exactly what her friend meant and she shook her head. "After what happened two years ago, ending this on my wedding day would be social suicide. No. I shall marry this man and somehow find a way to be happy with it."

Merritt still looked uncertain, but she reached over and took Vanessa's hand gently. "Then I will be at your side through it all."

Vanessa leaned her head on her friend's shoulder and sighed. At least there was that. And that had to be enough.

Benedict

Benedict entered Arthur's study, hoping to find his friend waiting there, making his final preparations before he married the beautiful woman Benedict had just left behind in the parlor. Only it wasn't Arthur sitting at the desk when he entered the room. It was Darrius.

He looked up at Benedict's entry and stiffened, his expression becoming dark and unreadable. It had been that way since the night of their unexpected encounter two years before. Their friendship had frayed, replaced by tension, and not the kind that led to pleasure.

That was, of course, unless they could pretend to be anonymous. Then sometime Darrius let the shield down. Let Benedict in.

"What is it?" Darrius snapped, sharp.

Benedict shook his head. This was not the time to ponder their relationship. He had a bad feeling and he needed to address it. "Where is he?"

Darrius clenched his fists against the top of the desk and his jaw flexed. He didn't ask Benedict for clarification on the he that they referred to. He just ground out, "I-I don't know."

The concern was so heavy in Darrius's voice that Benedict took a long step toward him. "When was the last time you saw him?"

"Last night," Darrius said softly. "When we had drinks with the Marquess of Egerton and his guest, Peter Reid."

Benedict nodded. "That was the last time I saw Arthur, as well."

He thought back to the exchange. It had seemed normal enough. They'd played billiards together and toasted the union. Benedict had been occasionally distracted by the intensity of the bond between the marquess and the celebrated playwright, Peter Reid. They never touched each other, but they were always circling, their energy connected.

"I don't recall anything off about him," Benedict continued.

Darrius got up and paced to the window to stare outside. "My brother has been acting oddly for a couple of months, but I assumed it was the reality of the marriage sinking in. I...I hoped it was him coming to terms with it, perhaps even looking forward to it. After all, he is incredibly lucky in his choice."

Benedict lifted his brows. There was a lilt of longing to Darrius's tone when he said that. And he understood it. Vanessa Gardner was a beauty, inside and out. It was impossible not to be drawn to her, body and spirit. Except he hadn't felt Arthur's draw to her in that way.

"Was that the same sense you got last night?" Benedict pushed.

Darrius faced him, bright blue gaze meeting his and holding there. "The last two days he's seemed more and more strange. And last night, after you three had gone and we were saying out good-nights, he...he shook my hand for far too long. And I'm realizing he said goodbye, not good night."

Benedict caught his breath. "Fuck," he whispered.

"Yes." Darrius pressed his full lips together. "But perhaps I am assuming the worst."

Darrius hadn't named what the worst was, but Benedict knew it. He nodded. "We shall have to hope so. Come, I'll help you look for him."

"No!" Darrius's voice was sharp, and Benedict stared at him even more closely.

"Are you doing this right now?" Benedict asked softly. "When there is an emergency? You'd let your personal feelings for me...or lack thereof...keep you from receiving the help you need from a person you know you can trust?"

Darrius's gaze flitted over him and then he sighed. "Fine. Yes. I would appreciate your help, Norfolk. Benedict."

Benedict sucked in a breath. Darrius hadn't called him by his first name for years. Now it felt like it mattered.

There was a knock at the door and both men jumped a little. Darrius looked past him as the butler, Turner, stepped into the study. "I apologize for intruding, gentlemen. Mr. Warwick, his lordship's valet found this note for you in the viscount's chamber a few moments ago."

He held out a missive, messily folded. Benedict sucked in a breath as he briefly saw the hand in which Darrius's name had been written. It was definitely from Arthur. His heart sank and his stomach turned.

"Thank you, Turner," Darrius said, his voice rough as he took the note. "Please be at the ready. I fear you will be needed a great deal today."

The butler looked concerned, but said nothing as he exited the room and quietly closed the door behind him. Darrius held up the note and shook his head. "This cannot be good."

"Read it," Benedict said, wishing he could reach out and squeeze Darrius's arm but knowing he would pull away if he did. "And we will face whatever comes next together."

Darrius gave a soft intake of breath and then he unfolded the note and read it. His frown turned farther and farther down as the seconds ticked by and the color left his face. Finally he lifted his gaze.

"He left," he explained, tucking the note away in his pocket without letting Benedict read it. "He ran off. And he wasn't alone."

Benedict shut his eyes and tried to meter his response. "With who?"

"With Vanessa—Miss Gardner's maid," Darrius said.

Benedict recoiled at that statement and the rush of realization of all the pain and disruption it would cause. Dear God, but Arthur had stepped in it. How could he be so idiotic when he had such a woman like Vanessa waiting to be his bride?

Vanessa. Benedict couldn't help but think of her as he'd left her a short time before. She was so beautiful and so light. He'd watched her in the six months since Arthur had announced his intention to wed her. In truth, he'd had almost as difficult time turning his gaze from her as he sometimes had turning it away from Darrius. So he felt desire for two people he couldn't have.

Darrius walked across the room back to his brother's desk and rested his hands on the top. He leaned over, his shoulders curled, his face stormy. Benedict restrained himself and stayed where he was, waiting for whatever Darrius would say next.

"Bloody hell, he is a fool," he breathed, and then slammed his hands against the desk. "A selfish, fucking fool."

Benedict didn't argue. "We must tell Miss Gardner," he said softly.

Darrius looked up at him and there was something in his expression that collapsed a little. "Yes. I know. Will you...will you come with me to do it?"

"Of course," Benedict said without hesitation. He sighed. "We can make it easier for her. She doesn't deserve this pain."

"No," Darrius said, his voice rough. "She doesn't. Come then. We shouldn't wait a moment more. She deserves to hear this news as soon as possible."

Benedict stared at this man, who had five times the decency and honor that his brother did. And cared about even more deeply, though his future with him was as dark and unreachable as Vanessa's future now was with Arthur. He had no idea how to untangle it all.

He feared perhaps they couldn't.

CHAPTER 2

Vanessa

Vanessa appreciated what Merritt was trying to do by sitting with her, holding her hand, chatting with her as if this was just another day and not one tinged with regret and worry and confusion. Merritt was older than she was by several years, but from the moment Vanessa had entered society, the marchioness had gathered her up and called her friend and offered her glimpses into worlds she longed to more fully explore.

Merritt tilted her head slightly and explored Vanessa's face. "I feel I would be remiss if I didn't offer my advice on your wedding night."

Vanessa's eyes went wide and she choked on her next breath. "I...you are offering to give me *the talk?*"

Merritt nodded. "I know it is the provenance of a mother on a day like this, but I have to believe she would do a terrible job of it. Tell you to lie there and think of your duty, all while she pulls faces of disgust. It wouldn't prepare you."

"You know I don't need it," Vanessa said, dropping her voice so no one would overhear that shocking fact. "I have already…done what I will do with Arnold…*Arthur* tonight."

Merritt pursed her lips. There were a few people in this world who knew Vanessa's secret, but only one was her champion, entirely on her side. The marchioness was that one.

"Perhaps it will be different," Merritt said, squeezing her hand.

Vanessa caught her breath and ducked her head. "No. He…he doesn't want me. He's made that very clear, even more so as the wedding date has neared. I am nothing more than an account to him, one that will be made available the moment he says *I do*."

"I'm sorry," Merritt said, and looked genuinely so. "I wanted more for you."

"Like what you have," Vanessa said, glancing up.

There was a knowing sensuality that entered her friend's eyes. "If you wanted that, I would love for you to have what I have."

Vanessa sighed. "Well, at least I can fantasize. Thanks in no small part to the books you sneak to me."

Now Merritt smiled in triumph. "I am very proud of how I've completely corrupted you and opened your eyes to pleasures beyond what society says is proper for a lady to desire. Did you enjoy the last book I shared with you?"

Vanessa's cheeks got hotter. "Yes, very much. I was quite scandalized by the idea of a lady with two gentlemen, as happens in part of the tale."

Merritt arched a brow. "Scandalized or titillated?"

"Take your pick. Sometimes it's hard to know the difference when I'm reading it."

Merritt drew a short breath and it seemed she was about to say more on the topic when the door to the parlor opened and Darrius Warwick, Arthur's younger brother, and Benedict Norfolk entered. Vanessa wished she hadn't been thinking about such scandalous things as she looked at them standing together, both as handsome as anyone could want a man to be.

But they did not look happy and she slowly rose to her feet. "What is it?"

The two men exchanged a brief look and then Mr. Warwick was the one who answered, "Miss Gardner, we need to speak to you and your parents."

As if on cue, Vanessa's parents hustled into the room behind the two men in a burst of dramatic flair. Her mother's hands fluttered around her head and her father was almost purple with what seemed to be anger.

"We have been looking all over, Mr. Warwick," he stormed. "Just where is your brother?"

"Yes! He has not been anywhere to be found," her mother all but sobbed. "He was to meet with us this morning and did not appear at the agreed upon time. Where are the manners in this family?"

Vanessa jerked her head toward them. They were having a clandestine meeting with her intended without inviting her? On her wedding day? Why?

"I will not stand for it, Mr. Warwick," her father continued, stepping up to the man with his finger in his face.

Warwick moved his head slightly away from the offending finger and glowered down at her father, his impossibly blue eyes narrowing. "*Sit down,*" he ordered.

Vanessa caught her breath at the calm command he lowered onto the room with those two words. Her father sputtered into silence, as did her mother, and that was a rare enough occurrence that Vanessa nearly smiled.

Except she couldn't, because whatever these two men were about to tell them all, it wasn't good. She reached back to catch Merritt's hand and clung there with all her might, wishing she could take a bit of her friend's fountain of strength.

"Lady Egerton, perhaps it would be better if you left," Warwick said.

Merritt gripped her hand tighter. "No. I will not leave her without protection."

"Merritt," Vanessa whispered, loving her friend for being her champion. Sometimes it felt like she was the only one.

"Please trust that the lady is not unprotected," Benedict Norfolk said, holding Vanessa's stare evenly. And strangely, she felt that protection in that moment. Felt the warmth that came from this man's steady presence.

"And there is us!" her mother screeched. "Lady Egerton, I resent your implication that…"

She carried on and Vanessa sighed, ignoring her as she turned to Merritt. "Perhaps…perhaps it is better if you left me with just them. It will potentially calm them down slightly."

Merritt frowned. "I don't want to leave you."

"I'll be fine," Vanessa assured her, even though it didn't feel true. "And I'll fetch you as soon as I know what is going on."

Merritt looked uncertain, but she gave Vanessa a brief hug before she glared at Warwick and Norfolk and left the room. Left Vanessa alone in this situation. She straightened her shoulders and drew a long, steadying breath for whatever would come next.

"Please, Mr. Warwick, Mr. Norfolk," she whispered. "What is it you must tell me that makes you both look so…so dire?"

Warwick returned his attention to her and she caught her breath. He had never looked at her directly before. He always glanced past her or over her and then away. She knew he didn't like her much, though she wasn't certain why. It made her own attraction to him all the more ridiculous. But now…now he held her entirely in his focus and there was an intensity to the feeling that made her knees a little weak.

"I do not know how to say this to soften the blow," he said evenly. "Or to ease the pain it will cause you, so I will just be direct. My brother is…he's gone. He left."

The words rang in her ears as she stared at him, trying to comprehend what he meant, what this meant for her. "How—how do you know?"

"He left a letter," Norfolk said before Warwick could answer, resulting in Warwick sending him a glare.

"He did," Warwick said softly.

She stepped toward him and held out her hand. "I want to see it."

He faltered, possibly for the first time since she'd met him. "I don't think that's a good idea."

"I wasn't asking your opinion on that score," she said. "I want to see the letter."

He pursed his lips and withdrew two folded sheets from his pocket. He removed the second one and handed out just the first to her.

"Please," she said. "Let me see it all."

He shook his head. "The second page was directed toward me. It wasn't about his leaving. What you want to see is in this part."

She sighed, because it was clear the man wouldn't be turned. She took the paper and examined it. She had to assume it was Arthur's handwriting. In that moment, she realized she'd never received a message from him during their entire courtship. It was sloppy and large and overfilled the page.

Darrius,

Unlike you, I cannot live a lie, not for all the money in the world. I'm leaving tonight to be with a person I care about and desire more than any woman I've ever met. Mary might be a maid and she might not bring anything but herself to our future, but it will be more than enough. Now as for you...

That was where the letter cut off, apparently continued on the page that Warwick...Darrius...hid from her. But Vanessa couldn't think about that, wonder about it. She read the words again, her head swimming.

"Hand it over, girl!" her father snapped, snatching the page from her hand.

She stared at Warwick. "He...he ran away with my maid? Is that what I understand? Your brother left me on our wedding day...with my maid, Mary?"

Warwick's nostrils flared and his jaw tightened before he let out a short nod. "Yes. I'm afraid that's exactly what has happened, Miss Gardner."

~

Darrius

If Darrius had expected Vanessa Gardner to collapse when she received the news of his brother's betrayal, he was shocked that she didn't do that at all. She only wavered slightly, a tiny buckling that she corrected before anyone could reach her to shore her up. She continued to stare straight ahead, straight into his eyes even as her parents began to wail and shout and make a huge fuss behind her.

Not for the first time, he noted how lovely her eyes were. They were such a warm dark brown, and filled with depths he'd been drawn to many a time in their short acquaintance.

"How could you let this happen *again*, Vanessa!" her father said, and that dragged Darrius out of the inappropriate study of the woman.

He moved forward and found that Benedict had done the same at his side. Vanessa's head dropped and her cheeks flamed brightly at the mention of the subject that no one ever spoke of. Her first engagement, which had also been broken two years before. It had been the talk of Society for a short time, especially when her first intended married another lady within weeks of the break.

His chest hurt a little with the realization that this second fracture would likely destroy her. And instead of her parents offering support, they were both glaring at her, pressing the weight of their own disappointments down on her slender shoulders.

"I do not know how I could have prevented this," she said softly. "I did not encourage the man to seduce my maid, I assure you of that."

Mr. Gardner moved another step toward his daughter, his hands clenched at his sides. "And yet you did nothing to keep the man, either. Even though you know what this means to your mother and me. You know what your *failure* will do to us."

She flinched at the word *failure*, even as she pushed her shoulders back farther. "You don't think this will hurt me, too, Father?"

"Selfish to the end," her mother interrupted with a huff.

And that was about as much as Darrius could take. "That is enough," he said, moving another step closer and putting himself partly in front of Vanessa. From the corner of his eye, he saw her glance up at him in surprise, but he ignored it. "If there is blame to be placed, then put it on my brother. *He* is the party that has wounded you, not Miss Gardner."

"Oh yes, I have a great many thoughts about your brother. But you have no idea," her father all but hissed. "No idea of her behavior, of how she gives not a damn about hurting her family, even though *we* are her only source of support."

Vanessa's breath became shorter and shorter as he spoke, and she stepped around Darrius at last, hands on her hips. "Then cut me off."

The room grew perfectly silent for a moment as everyone stared at her. Her eyes were filled with tears, her expression laced with pain that touched every element of his terrible situation and Darrius felt a drive to help her. Save her. Protect her.

"Don't tempt me," her father barked, and then he did the unthinkable: he caught her arm, dragging her roughly toward him.

Darrius lunged and found Benedict doing the same. Darrius grabbed for Mr. Gardner, catching his lapels and yanking him away from Vanessa. Benedict reached for her and guided her back a few steps, pulling her close to his side. Darrius tried not to look at them standing together, the two most beautiful people he'd ever seen, and focused instead on his pulsing rage toward Mr. Gardner.

"You will not touch her," he snarled, shaking the other man none too gently.

"She is my daughter, I will do what I like to punish her for her misdeeds," Mr. Gardner said, but the tone was weak. Apparently he didn't like being pushed around, only bullying others.

"There are no misdeeds to punish," Darrius said, and shoved him away, sending him spiraling toward his wife. "And you two will leave my home if you cannot cease this behavior and support your daughter."

The Gardners stood together a long moment, Vanessa staring at them, leaning toward her parents, as if willing them to do what was right for her. But her father only glared at her with such animus that it stung Darrius.

"You will get what you want, then. And good riddance." He pivoted and marched from the room. Mrs. Gardner lingered, but only for a moment, before she trailed after her husband without so much as a backward glance toward the daughter they were abandoning after she had been victimized.

Vanessa made a sound in the back of her throat that Darrius didn't think he would ever forget, it was so pained and wounded. She buckled a little, but this time Benedict was next to her and he caught her, drawing her against him gently. Darrius stared at them together again. That was best. He wasn't built to comfort. All he could do was his best to repair.

Not that he could think of a way to do that. He turned away. "I will find your friend, the marchioness."

He said nothing more, but left the room. Turner stood in the hallway, his face lined with concern and readiness to act. Darrius let out a sigh. "Mr. and Mrs. Gardner will be leaving us, I think, so be sure everything is ready for that inevitability. And when the guests arrive for the wedding, send them away."

"Sir?" Turner breathed, his eyes going wide.

Darrius shook his head. "The viscount has not behaved well. Give an excuse to try to protect Miss Gardner as long as we can. It will not be enough, but we must try."

"An illness in the family?" Turner suggested.

"Good man." Darrius squeezed his arm gently. "Do you know where the marchioness went after she left the parlor?"

"Lady Egerton joined her husband and their companion in the music room, I think," Turner said. "Shall I fetch them?"

"No, I will find her, thank you," Darrius said. He smoothed his jacket as he continued down the hallway to do just that. From what he'd witnessed in the parlor, he suspected the marchioness was a steadfast friend to Vanessa, but he still needed to be careful what he revealed when he found the lady.

The music room was at the end of the hall, and he opened the door quietly and stepped inside. He was surprised by what he found there. The marchioness was indeed there, with her husband, who Darrius had always considered a friendly acquaintance. She sat on the marquess's knee, his hand splayed against her thigh. That would have been an intimate enough image, but their companion, the playwright, Peter Reid, was also with them. He stood before the pair, knee pressed to Egerton's, Reid's hand resting against her shoulder and his gaze locked with hers.

Darrius jolted at the suggestive sight. He'd heard a few faint rumors about the relationship with the three. Whispers in the darkened areas of certain clubs that he frequented when he was wound too tightly. When he needed to stop pretending. But he hadn't seen them like this before.

And for a moment he found himself picturing himself in the marquess's place. With Benedict tucked up so close that their knees touched. And between them...well, he was shocked that his mind easily conjured Vanessa as the lady in the equation.

He cleared his throat and tried to clear his mind. Reid stepped away, almost casually, and the marchioness got to her feet. She didn't look embarrassed to be found in this way, nor did the marquess, who merely looked up at Darrius with an arched brow.

"How is she?" Lady Egerton asked.

He shook his head slightly and her expression fell. "It is not my story to tell, but I think Miss Gardner could use a friend."

"Oh no," Lady Egerton breathed, then reached back to squeeze her husband's hand before she hustled past Darrius and down the hall to rejoin Vanessa in the parlor.

Darrius remained at the door awkwardly, still watching Egerton and Reid. Egerton slowly got to his feet and moved closer, his dark gaze locked on Darrius. "Do you need something?" he asked.

Darrius swallowed. "No. It's been a very long morning."

"I assume so," Reid said. "Merritt filled us in a little on whatever she knew. Lady Egerton, that is."

Darrius looked between them. "Yes. Well. Yes. I ought to go take care of a great many things. But I assume you'll be staying and perhaps we can discuss this…something…later on."

He wasn't one to stammer and felt like a fool as the two men stared at him. But before the matter could be addressed, he turned away and headed back into the hall. His mind must be addled to be pondering erotic images in the midst of hell. He had to get himself together and not forget exactly why he couldn't pursue any desire that took hold of him, lest he become just as bad as his own brother.

Or worse.

CHAPTER 3

Vanessa

In the moments since Darrius Warwick had departed the room, leaving her alone with Benedict Norfolk, Vanessa had been fighting to keep control over her emotions. It was an almost impossible task, especially since the handsome man before her watched her with such a kind expression.

"I fear you must think me very silly," she gasped out.

He took a long step toward her, dark eyes going wide with surprise at that assertion. "Never. I think Arthur cruel and foolish. I think you brave and determined. Both of which are fine qualities, but also ones you do not need to exhibit in front of me at this moment. If you want to scream, scream. If you want to cry, cry."

Both those options seemed very good, but she didn't know him well enough to do either in front of him, despite how tempting it was. She shook her head. "Perhaps I'll drink instead."

She'd been half-kidding, but he moved to the sideboard across the room and dug around in the cabinet beneath for a bottle. He lifted it and sloshed the liquid within back and forth. "This is Arthur's finest whisky. He had it brought in from Scotland and he only allows it to be drunk on very specific occasions. I say we polish off the bottle. The bastard deserves it."

Vanessa had the strangest desire to laugh at that suggestion, but instead she moved to the settee and collapsed down on it. She watched Norfolk pour their drinks, marking how his body moved with such ease and grace even when doing such a simple act.

"Whatever he did, I know he is your best friend," she said. "You don't have to pretend to take my side against him, as kind as that may be."

He took a place on the opposite end of the settee and handed over a very full tumbler of liquor. "He *was* my friend, but not my best one, I assure you. Now he's…" He sighed. "After this, I cannot imagine ever calling him friend again. He has revealed himself to be thoughtless and cruel and I could not stand beside a man like that."

"Then *you* must be the very best of men, Mr. Norfolk," she said softly, and lifted her glass for a toast.

"Arthur creates a low standard, but I appreciate it," he said, and clinked his glass to hers. "I think you must call me Benedict if we are to be friends. I'm in the market for a new one, you know."

She smiled again. It was odd how easy he made it to do that, even in the midst of something so awful. Then she sipped the alcohol and stifled a cough at how strong it was.

"It isn't about being in love with him, you know," she said when she could speak again. "I was never in love with him."

"I know," Benedict said softly. "It was an arrangement, as many unions of our station are."

"But I had hopes that we could work something out," she whispered. "That it would be better once we'd said our vows and bound our lives. But…"

She shook her head. She didn't want to say more. She didn't want to be so vulnerable as to wonder out loud if any man could truly want her after two terrible experiences that had proven they might not. That felt a little desperate to share with so handsome a man, kind or not.

He leaned an arm on the back of the settee and his fingers flexed, like he wished to touch her, probably out of comfort. "Vanessa," he said softly, and she shivered at the sound of her name in his rough, low voice.

"Vanessa?" This time her name was said by Merritt as she stepped into the parlor.

Vanessa got to her feet and Merritt opened her arms. She crossed to the marchioness and let herself be folded into her embrace. She continued to cling to her glass of whisky even as she sobbed a little, able to be vulnerable with her dear friend as she hadn't been able with Benedict.

He got to his feet behind her and downed the rest of his drink. Then he crossed the room and smiled at her. "I'll leave you to your friend. But Vanessa, I swear to you, Warwick…Darrius and I…we'll make this right somehow."

She nodded even though she couldn't think of a way this could be made right. There was no way to march Arthur back to fulfill his promise. Even if they did, could she marry a man who had done this to her? Either way, it wouldn't be done before their wedding guests began to arrive and news of this humiliation began to spread.

He departed the room and Merritt guided her back to the settee. "Oh dearest," she whispered. "What happened?"

Vanessa drank another gulp of whisky and then she spilled out everything to Merritt, from Arthur's departure with Mary to the showdown with her wretched parents. "Do you think they truly left?"

The color in Merritt's cheeks bled away and she darted her gaze from Vanessa's. "I'm…I'm sorry, Vanessa. But as I was coming to you, I bumped into your mother's poor, harried maid. They *were* preparing to leave."

Vanessa had known they would. When she'd finally had the gumption to call her father out on his ceaseless threats and he had said he'd leave her, she'd seen his drive to do just that. But to hear that it was true. That it was really happening…

She bent her head against Merritt's shoulder once more and cried for a bit longer. Merritt said nothing, just stroked her hair until she could breathe again and she lifted her head with a shuddering sigh.

"What do I do now?" she whispered. "I've been left here by them with two men who have no allegiance to me. Benedict, Mr. Norfolk, is kind enough, but Arthur's brother doesn't even like me."

Merritt lifted both brows. "That wasn't the impression I got when he came into the room to find me. Nor when I have seen him look at you in the past."

Vanessa shifted. Darrius Warwick felt like a mystery to her. One she found herself pondering a bit too often truth be told. He often had an unreadable expression and when he focused it on her, his full lips pressed taut, she felt both uncomfortable and tingly. And then today he had stood up for her, almost out of nowhere.

She sighed and pushed those thoughts away. In this emotional state, it was not good to let her mind wander to such things.

"I should have known this would happen," she said softly.

"How could you have known?"

She lifted her gaze. "My mother and father encouraged me to keep certain aspects of my past a secret," she said.

Merritt pursed her lips. "That your first dastardly fiancé took your virginity?"

She nodded. "Yes. But I felt that was dishonest. So I...I wrote Arthur a letter two months ago, and I had Mary deliver it to him in secret."

Merritt's mouth dropped open. "Do you think that is when they began their affair?"

She shrugged. "I don't know. But after that, both their attitudes toward me changed. He had already been distant, but he became increasingly cold. And Mary became distracted, sharp. Why couldn't I see what was right before my eyes?"

"You are determined to blame yourself for this, but it is not your fault."

"It will be my consequences, though," Vanessa whispered.

Merritt couldn't argue that, so she merely pulled Vanessa in for comfort and squeezed her gently. "We're going to work this out. I won't rest until I know you are safe. I promise you."

Vanessa appreciated that promise. She knew her friend would do everything in her power to keep it. She just wasn't certain there was a good solution out there. Only pain.

Benedict

Benedict sat across from the Marquess of Egerton and Mr. Peter Reid in Arthur's office. Darrius was at the window, looking out with a grim expression. He'd been surprised to be asked into this meeting about Vanessa's future. He'd assumed Darrius would cut him out, as the emotions were high and that always made Darrius uncomfortable.

And yet he was here. And he couldn't help observing Egerton and Reid. He'd heard rumors about them. And about their relationship with the marchioness. But now, sitting across from them, watching the way the two men spoke to each other, moved with each other, there was no denying there was a connection between them.

He glanced again at Darrius and felt a tug of longing.

"I do not like to admit it," Darrius said with a shake of his head as he pivoted back to look at the three men. "But I am at a loss. My brother's behavior has shattered his own reputation, and potentially mine by proxy. He has no money to run the estate, which is the reason he was pressed to wed. If he doesn't return I don't know what will happen to those who depend upon it. And of course worst of it all is that he has dragged an innocent victim into this and materially damaged her. Miss Gardner doesn't deserve this."

Egerton nodded. "Even were she not one of my wife's dearest friends, I would wholeheartedly agree."

"Her parents have, unfortunately, abandoned her, as well," Darrius continued.

Peter Reid let out a sigh. "Yes, Merritt believes they will not change their mind on that score. They won't protect her in order to step away from blame and shield themselves."

Benedict pursed his lips in disgust at their cruelty. "Then *we* must protect her instead."

Darrius squeezed his eyes shut and his hands gripped at his sides. It was obvious he knew that was the only answer, as well. That they would all have to take some ownership of Vanessa's future. The others might not understand what that meant, but Benedict did. He had always been the closest observer of this man and he had seen the flutter toward Vanessa that Darrius tried to hide. The attraction to her was yet another thing they shared.

So what would Darrius do about it? What would Benedict?

Egerton was watching Darrius closely now, too. "Peter, would you and Mr. Norfolk go check in on Merritt and Vanessa?"

Peter arched a brow at him. "Right now?"

Egerton held the other man's gaze evenly, unspoken communication flowing between them. "Please." He said it so softly.

Peter nodded and got to his feet, pressing a hand to Egerton's shoulder. "Of course."

Benedict glanced at Darrius, but he was looking away. As if he didn't want to make the same connection that was so obvious between Peter and Egerton. He let out a ragged sigh and motioned toward the door as he got to his feet. "After you, Reid."

He glanced back before he went into the hall and now Darrius was watching him, gaze filled with torn emotions, anxieties and needs that he would never let Benedict fill. And it was such a loss.

～

Darrius

"I'm surprised you asked Reid to depart," Darrius said as he moved to the seat Benedict had occupied before he left. It was still warm and he gripped the armrests with both hands. "He seems to be of great import to you."

Egerton arched a brow. "Indeed, he is," he said softly. "As Norfolk seems to be to you."

"Norfolk is my brother's closest friend," he said with a dismissive shrug he'd practiced for years and never made feel true to his own heart. "And someone who is trustworthy."

Egerton was quiet for a long moment, but he never looked away from Darrius. "I've seen you, you know. In clubs. Certain clubs."

"I don't know what you're talking about." A slight incline of the head was Egerton's only response. Darrius shifted slightly. "At any rate, I'm not sure what talking about that will help in this situation."

"It doesn't seem entirely unlinked to me." Egerton folded his arms. "I am not trying to pry or damage or embarrass. How you view your life and those in it, what you do about feelings that you might have been taught were wrong, is your business. But I do understand. And I understand wanting to protect everyone around yourself."

Darrius examined his hands, clenched in his lap. The fact was that this man *did* understand, he thought. There was no doubt about it. Perhaps he was the only person who would. "How did you know what you...wanted?"

"All my life I felt pull toward..." Egerton tilted his head. "Would you allow me to be direct rather than dancing around the subject?"

Darrius glanced toward the door and when he saw it was firmly shut, he shrugged. "Direct is fine."

"From the first moment I discovered desire, I felt a draw toward both men and women. I squashed it, leaned around the edges of it, pretended away any encounter of my youth with men. And then I was betrothed to Merritt and it made it easier because I wanted her…want her…to distraction. Peter was a complication. I won't get into it, but he knew Merritt before she wed me. I pretended that he was a gift for her, a pleasure for her. But it became patently obvious that it wasn't true."

"And she could accept that?" Darrius asked, his voice raw.

"She embraces it." A hint of a smile crossed Egerton's normally serious face. "We complete each other. Him and me. Her and me. Him and her. Us. Together. Once they showed me the way, I couldn't walk away from either of them without losing a piece of myself." He looked toward the door. "How long have you and Norfolk pretended it away?"

Darrius pushed to his feet. "Norfolk is my brother's friend," he said roughly. "Nothing more."

"Very well." Egerton shrugged and also stood. "I do see how you look at Vanessa. How he looks at Vanessa. Perhaps there are solutions that would service her future, even if you never allow yourself to go as far as you'd like. And if not…" He sighed. "Then there are other options. Now I should find my wife…and our husband."

Darrius jolted at his use of that term and at the warmth with which Egerton said it. "Yes. Thank you for your help in this. Whatever happens, I know you could blame me without my brother being here to take the wrath."

"I would never blame a party that wasn't at fault." Egerton inclined his head. "We can speak more later if you'd like. Or we can go on pretending we don't know things about each other. Either suits me. Good afternoon, Mr. Warwick."

"Good afternoon," Darrius said with a shiver, as he watched a man who had embraced his heart…his desire…walk away. And burned with jealously.

CHAPTER 4

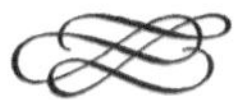

Vanessa

After a night of hiding in her chamber, eating with only Merritt as company and retiring to bed early so she could hide away from all that had happened in that long day, Vanessa couldn't sleep. She stared up at the canopy of the bed above her and let out a long sigh.

"Perhaps a book would help," she murmured to herself, and got up, pulling a wrap around her shoulders and heading into the silent hallway. The house was asleep now and she drew a long breath. She trusted Merritt, as well as Egerton and Peter Reid. And she liked Benedict a great deal. Warwick had said little to her, but he had defended her to her parents and not blamed her, himself. So she knew she was safe, at least physically, during her time here.

But the future still felt so very blurry. Dark. Frightening.

"Stop," she murmured, and stepped from the last step into the hallway downstairs. She flexed her hands open and shut, trying to get them to stop tingling. She was focused on that when she reached the library and pushed the door open a fraction.

She came to a complete halt at what she saw inside. Merritt was there, sprawled on the settee, a book on the floor beside her. But she wasn't alone. Peter Reid was perched between her legs, his tongue working her sex. Merritt's head rested on Egerton's lap and she was sucking his cock with long, smooth strokes. Egerton gripped a hand on the back of Peter's head, guiding him in pleasuring Merritt, but also toying with his hair as he watched and moaned.

Peter lifted his head and smiled. "Do you want to taste her?"

Egerton nodded with a groan, and Peter leaned up over Merritt to kiss the marquess passionately.

Vanessa was frozen, but then she realized what she was doing, standing there, intruding on a very private moment, and becoming aroused at the sight of it. She pivoted to rush from the doorway and crashed into the very firm chest of Benedict Norfolk. He was watching past her into the room and caught her arms to steady her. Their eyes met. His were dilated with desire but he said nothing, just covered her mouth with one hand and shut the door silently with the other.

He drew her down the hall, into the next open room. There was no fire within, so it was lit only by moonlight. They stood in a beam of it together, her looking up into his face as he drew his hand away from her mouth.

"I-I wasn't trying to spy," she whispered.

He shook his head. "I didn't think you were."

"What you must think of me," she whimpered. "After everything that happened today and now this."

She moved to walk around him, but he caught her hand, holding her in place. "I think we both stumbled into something we weren't meant to see. It's not your fault." He looked down her body and she was certain he could see her puckered nipples through her nightrail and thin dressing gown. His breath exited his lungs in a ragged sigh.

"Benedict," she murmured.

"What do you need?" he asked.

She swallowed hard. "What—what do you mean?"

He reached up and traced her cheek with his fingers. "I've

watched you since the first moment Arthur announced you would be his bride. I couldn't help it, even if it was wrong. And right now what I'd like to do more than anything is give you what you need."

She glanced toward the door. "I want...I want to feel wanted," she whispered, uncertain why the honesty had slipped from her lips, but not wanting to take it back.

His eyes went wide. "Wanted," he repeated.

She nodded.

"Like that?" he asked, nudging his head toward the door. He meant like Merritt had been wanted.

She shut her eyes, her mind creating errant images of being the woman at the center of such desire. "Yes," she whispered. "But I...I couldn't ever get one man to want me, at least not beyond a short while, let alone hope for two."

He stepped closer and his body heat was like a cloak in the cold room. She lost her breath as his hand moved to cup her chin and he tilted her face toward his. He lowered his lips slowly, as if giving her a chance to refuse him. To step away from this.

She couldn't. Her legs trembled as his mouth covered hers, gentle at first, then with more passion. His tongue traced her lips and she reached up to rest her hands on his shoulders. He tilted his head and then his tongue was inside, tasting and teasing. She met him thrust for thrust, moaning as sensation seemed to rush through her like water in a river.

He tugged her harder to his solid chest, wrapping his arms around her, letting her feel him from shoulder to groin. She wanted more. She wanted what she'd seen Merritt have. She wanted hands on her and mouths on her and someone to look at her like she was the center of the world. She wanted to have what the naughty books Merritt had shared claimed that one could find.

She wanted it all right now so that pleasure would wipe out the pain of the rest of the day. But he didn't push further, even though she felt the throb of his hard cock against her leg through his clothing.

He pulled away from her and shook his head. "Don't be so sure of that, Vanessa." He took her hand. "Come now, it's late and you've had a very long day. I'll take you upstairs and leave you before we do something we both regret tomorrow."

"You would regret it?" she whispered.

"If you only did it because you were upset and angry and needing to forget, yes. I think I would. I do want you to know, though, that you are very much wanted. And not just by me."

She blinked, uncertain she knew what he meant. She released his hand. "I'll—I'll take myself upstairs. Thank you...thank you for today, and for this. Whatever happens next, I do appreciate it."

He inclined his head and she raced from the room and back upstairs to her chamber. Inside, she threw herself on the bed, yanking the covers over her head, but she couldn't hide from herself. She could still taste him on her lips, still feel him on her skin. Oh God, but she wanted that. Wanted him. Wanted more.

She closed her eyes and lowered her hand, shoving her nightrail out of the way. And then she touched herself as she thought of Benedict, thought of what she'd seen in the library, thought of... Darrius Warwick. Her eyes flew open as an image of his handsome face loomed into the middle of the passionate fantasy. Both men, focused on her as her body began to spasm with pleasure. And those images remained with her even as she collapsed in relief against the pillows and drifted into restless dreams of even more wicked things the two of them could do to her.

Darrius

Darrius had never believed he would sleep that night. He hadn't even tried, instead dismissing his valet and returning to his brother's study where he began to go through every paper and ledger on Arthur's messy desk. What he was finding was such a pattern of mismanagement and irresponsibility that it made his head hurt.

He was about to get up and pour himself a drink when the door to the study opened and Benedict stepped inside. Darrius watched him a moment, outlined in the glow of the lamps and firelight. By God, but he was beautiful. Like a beacon in the darkness that was currently Darrius's life. He wanted so much to get up, cross the room and just…surrender himself to everything he'd ever wanted. He let his gaze flit over Benedict and hesitated when he realized the other man had what looked like half a cockstand.

And his mouth watered. But he blinked and shook away the reaction. There was no wasting time on such things now. "Do you not know how to knock?" he asked, his voice harsh.

Benedict ignored the question and entered the room, shutting the door behind himself. "I have an idea. A potential solution."

Uneasiness filled Darrius at the way he said that. "It's late, Benedict. I'm tired."

Benedict's lips pursed. "Are you so incapable of being around me for five minutes that you won't even listen to me? That you can't allow that I have your best interest at heart? Hers, too? That I might actually be useful to you as a friend?"

Darrius stared at him for what felt like a lifetime, then swallowed. "I know all that. I know…I know." He shook his head and thought of what Egerton had said to him hours before about his relationship with Reid and Merritt. "It's complicated, though."

Benedict stepped closer. "Because you make it so. Because you don't want to face…" He trailed off. "I'm not here to talk about that, actually. Or not exactly. Can't you just forget the so-called complications and *listen* to me?"

Darrius motioned toward the seat across from the desk. "Please."

Benedict sat and leaned forward, draping his elbows on his knees. His eyes shone in the light, his face lit up in a way Darrius hadn't seen in a long time. "Vanessa will have to marry."

Darrius flinched. That had been the path of his own mind, as well. "Yes. She cannot be unprotected."

"And it makes sense that it will be one of us," Benedict continued.

Darrius got up and moved to the fire, staring into the dying flames as he pictured Vanessa coming toward him. As much as he longed for Benedict, he couldn't deny that he had felt the same stirrings of desire and interest toward his brother's fiancée. He'd hated himself for it, had tried to avoid her just like he avoided Benedict.

It had worked just as well, for now he was here, with both the objects of his desire right before him, tempting him. What would marriage to her be like? Would she despise him for forcing her into a path like her parents had tried to do not once but twice? Would she feel trapped?

Would she come to care for him and ask for the same in return? Could he give that knowing that he still throbbed and would always throb for the man who sat behind him, waiting for him to respond?

Except Benedict wasn't just waiting. Darrius heard him get up and move toward him. He gripped the edge of the mantelpiece as Benedict stepped up behind him, close now. He could almost feel his breath and sucked in one of his own in anticipation.

"But she doesn't want something empty, Darrius. She doesn't want something cold," Benedict said, his voice becoming more seductive. "She wants to be wanted. Desired." Darrius felt Benedict's fingertips brush along his hip. "Pleasured."

He swallowed hard and turned slightly toward him. "How could you possibly know that?"

Benedict didn't step back, he didn't stop tracing the line of Darrius's hip, but he didn't surge forward and demand anything else, either. "You know that the Marquess and Marchioness of Egerton are involved in a relationship with Peter Reid."

Darrius sucked in a breath. "Y-Yes. I'd heard the rumors in certain corners. And Egerton verified it was true when I was talking to him this afternoon. What does that have to do with Vanessa?"

"I caught her in the hallway a short time ago, watching them as they...*indulged* in the library together," Benedict said, and now his breath came shorter, too. As if he was recalling what he'd seen and was aroused by it.

Darrius was, too. The idea of Vanessa and Benedict standing in a hallway not ten paces away from this very study, watching something so intimate, so passionate—it set his body on edge.

"I know you want her, Darrius," Benedict continued, and now he did lean forward, his lips close to Darrius's jawline. "I know when you want. And you know the same about me, so you must have guessed that I want her, too."

Darrius jerked his gaze to him, their faces too close. He was getting dizzy with the proximity, with the heat this conversation created. He gripped the mantel tighter and nodded. "Yes."

"So why couldn't we...share her?"

It was like someone had thrown a bomb into the middle of the room. Darrius staggered a little, but Benedict didn't allow him time to recover his senses, he just continued on.

"We could give her all the pleasure, all the adoration, she deserves after what she's gone through. Show her that she is wanted, despite the idiot men who came before us. And when she's had her fill, we've had our fill, she can pick between us for a husband, knowing full well what her future would look like instead of having it thrust upon her as has happened before."

Darrius knew that Benedict accentuated the word *thrust* and he glared at him for it. Benedict was spinning a plan that involved every single thing Darrius wanted. A careful seduction meant to give Darrius no choice but surrender. He started to step away, but Benedict caught his arm. He dragged him closer, their chests colliding.

"I know what you want, Darrius. You know, too. Are you going to run away like you always do?" He lifted a hand and slid his fingers into Darrius's hair. "Or are you going to allow this? For her. For you. For me."

Darrius wanted to grab him. To kiss him on the mouth, something he'd never done before. He'd back him across the room, onto the desk, and take Benedict in his mouth. To bend him over the same desk and take his arse until they were both writhing in pleasure.

But instead he stepped away. Benedict released him this time, watching as he went back to the desk and sat down. At least his own cockstand wouldn't be so obvious now.

"Have you ever considered that this might be too far for *her*?" Darrius asked. "Wanting to be desired or not, the lady is likely an innocent. Watching something erotic and doing it are two different things."

"Then why don't we ask her?" Benedict said.

Darrius snapped his mouth shut at the suggestion. One he had no way to deny. Vanessa had spent her life having no say in what happened to her, the exchange with her hideous parents had proven that. He couldn't be so cruel as to deny her all the options for her future now.

"Fine," he ground out. "We will bring the subject up tomorrow… *delicately*."

The heat that leapt to Benedict's eyes was so intense that Darrius was glad he was sitting down because he was certain he would have gone weak in the knees.

"Now I'm going to bed," Darrius said, and got to his feet.

Benedict didn't move. "Yours or mine?"

"Mine," Darrius replied, and looked away from Benedict. Benedict snorted a humorless laugh and turned away, but before he could leave the room and end this charged conversation, Darrius called out, "Benedict?"

He turned back, almost hopeful. "Yes?"

"If we do this…share her…it will be about her. Not each other."

Some of the pleasure left Benedict's expression and he pursed his lips. "That seems a shame, Darrius, potentially for everyone involved. But I've never forced you to do anything. I won't start now."

He left then, without so much as a farewell, and Darrius leaned back in his chair, letting his head hit the rest with a thud. Benedict was correct in what he'd said. In the years since their first passionate encounter in Darrius's old room in London, he had never pushed. Never asked for more. But he had certainly forced Darrius in ways he feared to name. Forced him to want. Forced him to long.

Forced him to bind up his aching heart so he didn't do anything that might break his world.

CHAPTER 5

Vanessa

The next afternoon, Vanessa had considered sitting in the library. It was a beautiful room, after all, with many interesting books. Only when she peeked in, she'd only been able to look at the settee where she'd witnessed the erotic sight of Merritt with her men. She couldn't sit here and pretend away her arousal and curiosity.

So she'd retreated to a small parlor on the other end of the hallway and now she sat in a chair before the fire, trying to focus on needlepoint, but unable to complete a row of stitches without having to pick them all loose and start again.

"An inauspicious start," she grunted.

She tossed the needlepoint aside at last and got up to go to the window. Outside, Merritt, Egerton and Mr. Reid were all loading into a carriage to go to the village for the afternoon. It was something Vanessa hadn't been able to do, herself. Too many eyes would be watching, too many whispers would happen when everyone knew she was supposed to have married yesterday.

And honestly, even if that hadn't been true, Vanessa wasn't

certain she could manage being alone with her friend and her two lovers. Even now, as Vanessa watched from above, Merritt was smiling as Egerton helped her up into the rig, his gaze following her every move. Vanessa shook her head and pivoted away from the image only to find Benedict and Mr. Warwick coming into the parlor together.

Heat rushed to her face immediately. After all, the two of them had been the subjects of her most wicked fantasies the night before. "Oh, good—good afternoon," she stammered.

"Good afternoon," Mr. Warwick returned first, his bright blue gaze sliding over her from head to toe before he dropped it away.

"Vanessa," Benedict said with a warmer expression, kinder, but still sharp and focused on her.

She had to be imagining things to feel their regard so strongly. She shook away the inappropriate reactions and stepped closer. "I must thank you, yet again, Mr. Warwick, for allowing me to stay here a little longer. I have no idea what my future holds, but not having to make every decision immediately is a great relief."

Benedict exchanged a brief glance with Warwick and tilted his head. "That is...that's why we've come to speak to you this afternoon, Vanessa. That very future."

"Very well, Benedict." She blushed as she glanced toward Warwick. "Er, Mr. Norfolk."

"You may call me Benedict in front of him," Benedict said, sending a meaningful look toward the other man. "Isn't that right, *Darrius?*"

Warwick hadn't stopped looking at her even during the exchange and he took a long step toward her. He really did have the most remarkable eyes, though they were entirely unreadable in that moment. Well, not entirely. There in the depths was a heat that made her heart flutter a little in her chest.

"I think, considering what we are about to discuss, first names would be appropriate." He extended a hand, as if they were meeting for the first time. "Darrius."

"Darrius," she repeated as they shook, and she saw his pulse quicken in his neck. "Vanessa."

He released her hand and walked away, toward the window where she had been standing not a moment before. He leaned back there, arms folded and nudged his head toward Benedict, as if to encourage him to begin. Benedict shot him a look in return, but then focused on her.

"Now that you've had a day to come to terms with the shock of Arthur's behavior," Benedict said gently. "Now that his foolhardy actions have sunk in for all of us, you must have thoughts. Worries."

"Of course," Vanessa said on a sigh. "I'm not a ninny." She glanced toward Darrius again, her cheeks heating once more. It was odd how much she wanted him to believe that. To not see her as a fool, though she was a bigger one for wanting the regard of a man who could hardly look at her for more than a moment at a time. "And I suppose I cannot pretend that this is the first time I've been abandoned by a fiancé at almost the last moment. I seem to be entirely unmarriageable. Unwantable."

She said the word and wished she could take it back. She'd said something similar last night to Benedict and he had kissed her thoroughly as response. Now in the bright light of day, with Darrius standing by, now watching with such intensity, that felt like revealing something.

Benedict shifted, but before he could speak, Darrius came forward. "The idea that you are unwantable is entirely ridiculous," he said, his tone a bit sharp. "You are most certainly wanted."

Her eyes went wide as she stared at him. Did he mean by himself? Even though he always behaved as though he didn't like her, always avoided her? Or was he referring to Benedict? Had he told Darrius about what had happened between them in the hallway?

"And marriageable," Benedict added. "But we cannot deny that what has happened with Arthur, added to what happened before with your prior engagement, will certainly create unpleasant talk. And so you must marry to mitigate the damage. Quickly."

She folded her arms. "Wonderful. I'll just move to the next name on my overflowing list of suitors. Let's see…that would be…no one. Who would you two have me marry?"

"One of us," Darrius said softly.

She stumbled a step and nearly put herself on her backside on the parlor floor. "One of you?" she repeated. "That's ridiculous."

"Why?" Darrius continued. "My brother is the one who wounded your future—I would be remiss not to offer a remedy."

"And he was my friend," Benedict added. "I ought to have been more aware of his dastardly plans. So I also must offer for you as a solution, as well."

Must. Remiss. Not exactly romantic notions from what appeared to be not one but two proposals. She frowned and bent her head. "I've been nearly forced into two marriages. I won't do the same to someone else."

"Just because something is arranged doesn't mean it's forced," Benedict said, coming to stand before her. He slid a finger beneath her chin and tilted it up so that she had to look into his dark eyes. "Or that it couldn't be vastly pleasurable for all parties involved."

She caught her breath and glanced at Darrius, shocked that Benedict would be so forward in front of him. But instead of looking uncomfortable or irritated, the other man was staring and for once she *could* read his expression. He looked…aroused. By watching her with Benedict.

Once again she thought of those wicked moments between Merritt, Egerton and Peter on the settee in the library. Why did she keep getting these men tangled in those ideas?

"You ought to be able to make this choice," Benedict said. "Knowing all the benefits and disadvantages you will find in a future with either of us."

She stepped back and he dropped his hand to his side as she shook her head. "And how exactly would I do that?"

"I know what you and Benedict saw last night," Darrius said, pushing off the window ledge and coming across the room toward her in a few long strides.

Now she stopped breathing entirely as she stared at him, humiliation overwhelming her. She glanced toward Benedict. "How—how could you tell him that? Why would you?"

His lips pinched. "It wasn't to hurt you, Vanessa, I promise. I..." He looked at Darrius. "Do you not know that both of us desire you?"

Vanessa's ears began to ring at those words and she turned away from Benedict toward Darrius. "You—you don't want me. You don't even *like* me."

His eyes went wide and there was a moment that stretched between them. Then he moved closer and reached out. His ungloved hand took hers and she shuddered at the warmth of him. The presence of him looming above her, holding her captive with the unending blue depths of his stare.

"If I have behaved distantly, that was not because I didn't like you," he said. "It was exactly the opposite. I coveted you, and I could not allow it when my brother was to be your husband. But he's gone now, Vanessa. He's gone and what is left is how I...how I *burn* for you."

Her lips parted at that heated declaration from a man who had only ever been chilly. She heard Benedict make a soft noise from beside them and found he seemed as moved by this statement as she was.

"What you saw last night must have shocked you," Darrius continued. "But Benedict told me that it also...interested you. That you told him you wanted to feel something similar. Could that be true? As an innocent, do you really know what that means."

She bent her head. "You think me an innocent?"

"Are...are you not? Did my brother do even worse than—"

"Not your brother," she hastened to say, and looked from one of them to the other. "You are saying I must know what I'm getting into with your offers, so I suppose it is only fair for you to know the same."

Benedict's expression gentled. "Very well. Tell us."

"Before, years ago, when I was engaged to the Earl of Avebury..." She struggled to continue.

"You don't have to tell us," Darrius said with a sharp look for Benedict.

She pushed her shoulders back. "If we are discussing a potential future, whatever that might entail, I think I do. Everyone knows that Avebury broke our contract. But he also...he...he convinced me that we didn't have to wait. That since we would be married, we could give in to whatever desire was between us." She squeezed her eyes shut. "Like a fool, I allowed it. And then he found a daughter of a duchess who would raise his fortunes and reputation even higher and walked away from me as if I were nothing."

Darrius's face twisted in disgust. "I have always despised that man, but never more than now."

She blinked at the passion of that statement. It reminded her of when he had come to her defense with her parents. It made her feel a little safer. So she had to tell them the rest. Let them know exactly what kind of woman she was so that she could truly understand what they were offering.

"In addition," she said, "Merritt has been sneaking me the most erotic books for almost a year."

Darrius's eyes went wide. "I-I see."

"They are very descriptive," she admitted with what she knew was a fierce blush. "And some have illustrations. So I am not so innocent. But somehow I still cannot comprehend what you two are offering me? Are you saying you would share me? Like Merritt is shared between Peter and Egerton?"

Benedict nodded. "If you would like that, yes, that is what I'm suggesting. That we would worship you, Vanessa. Pleasure you. Give you relief from the pain that has been caused by Arthur. While we were at it, you could get to know us better. As lovers and as people. When it was all over, this fantasy separate from reality, you could choose which man you would take as husband, thus protecting you from at least some of the censure Arthur's behavior will cause." He glanced at Darrius. "Isn't that right?"

Darrius looked at him now, with as much focus and heat as when he looked at her. She realized in that startling moment, that just like Egerton and Peter…Darrius and Benedict seemed to want each other, as well. What was even more surprising was that the idea of it was as titillating as the thought of their hands running over her, making her weak with pleasure.

This offer was outrageous and if she didn't feel so entirely awake and aware, she might have thought she was still dreaming. But these two men were here, they *were* suggesting this. She pinched herself to verify it.

"We have shocked you," Benedict said.

She nodded. "*Surprised*, I suppose, is a better word for it. I couldn't have thought that when I began this morning that this would happen."

"But do you want it?" Benedict asked. "Because that is the only thing that matters. Forgetting about potential marriages in the future, forgetting about everything else…do you want this?"

"And you don't have to have an answer yet," Darrius said, sending a hard glance at Benedict.

She worried her hands before her. "I appreciate it that Mr… Darrius. But I-I do have an answer. Last night after what we saw, I will admit that I pictured myself in the same position as my friend. Only it was…I was…you two were the men I imagined touching me." She bent her head, feeling her cheeks burn with the confession. "I want something wanton and wild and purely of sensation. I want something that is about pleasure, not pain. There has been too much pain as of late. So yes, I want this."

"Very good," Benedict said, his voice a little shaky as he moved to the window and closed the curtains. She watched him as he walked to the door and locked it. "Darrius, kiss her."

Darrius looked back over his shoulder at him, a glint in his blue eyes. But he didn't argue, he merely took Vanessa's hand and drew her closer. "May I?"

She nodded, unable to get enough air to speak, and for the second time in as many days, she watched a man's lips lower toward her own. She closed her eyes and then he was kissing her. But it wasn't gentle. It wasn't chaste. It wasn't exploratory. Darrius Warwick kissed her like he was hungry and she was a feast spread before him. Like he couldn't survive without her.

Like she was already his.

His big hands gripped at her back, his tongue warred with hers, and he made a deep, rumbling sound of pleasure from deep in his throat that made her entire body tingle with sensation. This was happening and she was undone by the power of him, of them, of the anticipation of pleasures like nothing she'd felt before.

CHAPTER 6

Benedict

There were many things about Darrius that Benedict had found arousing over the years and yet none of them were as powerful as watching him kiss Vanessa. He did so with gusto, abandon that he normally didn't allow and she returned that desperate heat with her own. They were well matched and beautiful, and Benedict wanted to touch them both until there was nothing left in the world but this.

He moved toward them slowly, dragging his fingertips along her forearm when he reached them. She let out a gasping moan against Darrius's lips, partially breaking the kiss. Darrius fully broke it and gently turned her toward Benedict, an offering of a goddess. She fell into him, lifting to him as if it were the most natural thing in the world.

In this moment, it was. He slid a hand into her hair, partially drawing it down as he tilted her head and kissed her. Was that Darrius's taste on her tongue? He wouldn't know. He'd never been allowed the pleasure. Any encounter between them, in secret or not, hadn't involved kissing, at least not on the lips.

He doubted this one would either, so he put all his energy into kissing Vanessa instead, measuring all her reactions just as he had the night before. When he drew back she stared up at him with a slightly bleary expression, like she'd had been taken by surprise.

"We aren't going to take you," Benedict said softly as he backed her to the settee and helped her settled onto the velvet cushions.

"Aren't we?" Darrius asked, his tone a bit amused. "I don't think I agreed to that."

"When we *do* take her," Benedict said with a brief glance to the other man, "it will be in a room where there is no chance of interruption. When we can take all night to make her ready for us."

Vanessa made a garbled sound in her throat and Darrius shivered—obviously the description had moved both of them as much as it moved Benedict.

"Then what should we do to her?" Darrius asked, his tone low and hypnotic now.

"I want you to make her come," Benedict said softly as they locked eyes and a thousand desires and secrets flowed between them. This was the connection he'd always longed for with Darrius. His voice shook as he said, "I want to watch her come for you."

Vanessa was breathless as she looked back and forth between them. "Do I get a say in this?"

Darrius glanced down at her, sprawled on the settee cushions, still appearing a little stunned by what was happening. "Do you not want this?"

"I want it," she said without hesitation. The enthusiasm made Benedict all the more excited at the prospect.

"Then let me," Darrius said, and to Benedict's surprise, he made no further argument against pleasuring her. He seemed more than willing to obey, at least in this.

If only Benedict could make him bend in other ways.

He took a place beside Vanessa on the settee and drew her against his side. They watched together as Darrius dropped to his knees before her. There was a little smirk that tilted his lips, rare and hot and filled with promises. He eased forward and wedged himself between her legs. She whimpered as he pressed one big hand against either thigh, leaning up to kiss her once again. She had been sitting stiffly, but now she relaxed, as if Darrius's kisses were drugging. Benedict wished he could partake, get lost in this man, in this woman.

Soon enough. He had to be patient.

He wrapped an arm around her and drew her to lean against him. Darrius opened his eyes even as he continued to kiss her and looked up into Benedict's face. This wasn't just for her, Benedict realized. This was a performance for *him*. Darrius was seducing him as much as the woman who gasped against him.

Darrius gave a small shiver, then pulled away from her mouth. He held her gaze as he slid his hands down her sides, her hips, down to the hem of her skirt. He began to push the fabric up her calves, revealing pale pink stockings incasing her long legs. Benedict stared, watching Darrius's big hands stroke over her ankles, her knees, her thighs as he pushed her skirt higher and higher.

Her breath was short now and she squirmed against Benedict. The movement shocked him into action and he unfastened the top button of her gown, the second, the third. The pretty fabric gaped and he pushed it forward a little, just enough to wedge one hand into the bodice, beneath her chemise.

She gasped as he brushed her nipple with his fingertips, circling the already taut nub. And the gasp turned to a cry when Darrius pushed her legs farther apart. He glanced up with a wicked smile for Benedict. "She's not wearing drawers."

Benedict's cock throbbed at that news and he tilted Vanessa's face toward himself. She bit her lip and it was too much. He dropped his mouth to hers and began to kiss her, just as Darrius lowered his head between her legs and licked her.

Vanessa

Vanessa's head spun, her world turned upside down by the two men who touched her, pleased her. Darrius's tongue was hot against her flesh, licking the length of her sex over and over, her sensitive body lighting on fire with every stroke. And as if that weren't overwhelming enough, Benedict sat beside her, her body half draped over him and his fingers were pressed to her breast. He plucked one nipple, then the other, and stroked her flesh as he kissed her.

She had never felt so alive, so on fire, so filled with need and desire as she did in that moment. Everything else faded away, all the pain of the last few days, all her confusion about her future, all her uncertainty about what these two men had offered. All that was left was exactly what they'd both promised: pleasure.

"Please," she whispered, and Darrius lifted his eyes, his fingers tightening against her thighs. They pressed into her skin, marking her and she wanted it.

He began to swirl his tongue around her clitoris slowly, round and round. There was so much focus to this man. From the way he was touching her, to the way he looked at her, to the way his tongue pressed against her with purpose.

"Yes," Benedict breathed, and she looked up at him. His expression was taut with tension as he watched Darrius at his work. His fingers began to mimic the other man's tongue, flicking around her nipples in slow circles.

She lolled her head against his shoulder, groaning as the warring pleasure hit her from all sides. She arched, rolling her hips against Darrius's tongue, forcing her breast into Benedict's fingers harder.

Darrius moaned against her sex, as if her excitement pleased him and the vibration began the last swirling climb to release. She was out of control now, arching and grinding for her pleasure, rocking against one man then the other. And at last, the sensation peaked, and she cried out, the sound captured by Benedict's mouth as she came.

Her entire body convulsed with the power of the pleasure, rolling through her in wave after ceaseless wave. Darrius held her steady as he continued to lick her through it, Benedict kissed her until she couldn't think or breathe or do anything but roll with the sensation that seemed to go on forever.

She had come before, both with her own hand and with her first fiancé, the man who had taken her innocence. But it had never been like this, this shattering that felt like she had been entirely remade.

Slowly the intensity faded and she gasped with relief as she went limp in Benedict's arms. He chuckled, his voice rough, and then looked down at Darrius, still perched between her clenching thighs. "That was even better than I thought it would be."

Darrius nodded, lifting his head from her sex and revealing lips that shone with her release. She wanted to lick them clean. She wanted to taste her own flavor and then start all over again.

"Was that what you needed?" Benedict asked her.

She shivered at the question and gave a shaky nod. "Yes."

Darrius pushed to his feet. There was no denying the outline of his hard cock through his tight fawn breeches. She wanted to touch him, draw him down to cover her, fill her. Then let Benedict do the same. She wanted to ride this pleasure forever, never stop, forget all her responsibilities and just be theirs until the world stopped turning. But he caught her hand and bent over her, kissing her knuckles lightly.

"There is nothing I want more than for you to touch me," he said, as if he could read her mind. "And to watch you be touched by Benedict. But the chances of our being caught this way increase with every passing moment. And I want you to have time to truly consider what we've done. If it is truly something you want to take further. To take all the way."

She blinked at the generosity of that offer. This man who had always seemed so indifferent was only thinking of her. Her pleasure. Her future. Her desire. Her consent. How had she ever believed he didn't like her when he looked at her like he was right now? With such gentleness, but also such heat. It had always been there, she realized it now.

Benedict turned her face toward his again and kissed her gently. "He's right."

"So take the time," Darrius whispered. "And if you want more… both of you…come to my room after everyone else turns in tonight. You'll have everything you desire and more."

She felt Benedict draw in a short breath, as if that promise moved him, but he didn't reveal his reaction on his face. He just kissed her one last time and then went about the work of helping her fix herself so that what they'd done wouldn't be so obvious when Darrius opened the door and let the world back into the parlor.

But inside she'd always know that she'd been changed. No matter what happened next.

Darrius

Darrius burst from the house and down the stairs from the terrace to enter the garden. He could scarcely breathe as he rushed down the pathway, not seeing the well-manicured greenness around him that often gave him peace. Today there was none of that. Not after the encounter with Benedict and Vanessa.

He could still taste her on his tongue, her desire and release both sweet and salty. And he could still feel Benedict's stare hold his, a thousand needs and feelings and thoughts Darrius had avoided sparked by that intimate exchange.

"Wait!"

He froze on the path and looked back to see Benedict coming after him in a few long, graceful strides. Darrius pinched his lips. "I thought we'd agreed to go to separate corners to consider what just happened?"

Benedict scrunched his face. "Vanessa has the most to lose. *She* must consider. I think we both know that for us, it's easy."

Darrius shook his head. They had danced around this topic for years now and it felt impossible to continue to do so after what had just happened. Or maybe he just didn't want to anymore.

"For *you*, it's easy," he snapped, emotions bubbling to the surface. "You always make it look so fucking easy. For me, it's not."

Expression falling, Benedict took another step toward him. "Why?"

"Because...because..." When Benedict was looking at him like that, heat flowing between them...something deeper than heat, too...he almost couldn't remember why. He shook his head. "I have responsibilities."

"So do I," Benedict said softly. "One of them is to be as authentically myself as I can be. The alternative is untenable. And perhaps I cannot run through the street declaring my—" He cut himself off, and for a moment Darrius wished he would have completed the sentence. "When it is you and me, you can be who *you* are. Don't you want that?"

Darrius sighed. "And what if *she* doesn't want that?"

As he ran a hand through his hair, Benedict turned away a moment. When he looked back, there was a flash of anger in his eyes. "You said earlier that we could have everything we desire and more. Well, you know what I desire, Darrius. What I've always desired. So don't pretend you don't."

Darrius scrubbed his palm over his face. "I—"

"Don't say anything." Benedict snapped. "But perhaps that is what *you* should think about while we wait for tonight. Because I can't play games with you anymore. I can't accept anonymous encounters in dark halls where you can pretend it away afterward. I need more."

With that, he turned away and left Darrius staring after him. And longing, as he always had longed and probably always would long, when Benedict Norfolk walked away from him.

CHAPTER 7

Vanessa

It had been two hours since the shocking encounter on the settee in the parlor and Vanessa had been pacing her chamber ever since. She could think of nothing else, imagine nothing else, remember nothing else but Benedict's hands on her, Darrius's mouth on her. Strange since she had been abandoned almost at the altar barely twenty-four hours before. Thoughts that humiliation should have been more forefront of her mind.

What a gift that they were giving her.

There was a light knock on her door and she rushed to it, almost pulling it from its hinges as she opened it. Merritt was outside, her face lined with concern. "When we arrived back, Turner said you needed me, what—"

Before she could finish the question, Vanessa grasped her hand and tugged her into the room, closing and locking the door behind her.

"Are you well?" Merritt asked, her tone growing sharper and more concerned.

"Yes. More than well. Or...I'm not sure." Vanessa shook her head.

"My mind is spinning and you are the only person I can talk to about it. The only one who could ever understand."

"Oh, my dear, this is such a difficult time, I know. And of course, I am here for you to vent to or plan with when it comes to your future. We will work it out." Merritt's eyes narrowed. "And if I can do anything to destroy Lord Warwick, I will do it."

Vanessa blinked. "No. Oh, this isn't about Arthur or any of that. At least, not directly."

Merritt pointed to the chairs before the fire with one hand and they each took one. "What then?"

Vanessa shifted her weight, worrying her hands in her lap. It was one thing to plan to say this out loud and another to do it, even to a woman who had a sense of erotic freedom that most ladies of her station didn't admit to. Her cheeks burned as she mustered all her courage.

"Benedict and Darrius..." She shook her head. "Mr. Norfolk and Mr. Warwick..."

Merritt's eyes went wide. "Yes?"

"They have offered me a...well, a...they've suggested that we could..." Merritt leaned forward to the edge of her seat, nodding in encouragement. Vanessa shut her eyes so she wouldn't have to look at her. "Have an affair. The three of us. Together. Like...like you do with Egerton and Mr. Reid."

She opened one eye to peek at Merritt. She had leaned back in her chair again with a slightly knowing smile. "You figured that out, did you? At last?"

Vanessa's cheeks burned hotter. "I-I saw you. Briefly. In the library."

Merritt burst out a bark of laughter and now her cheeks pinkened. "I told Elliot that he should lock the door. He got carried away and dragged Peter and I right along with him, as he is wont to do."

"How did it happen?"

"The library or the life?" Merritt asked.

Vanessa smiled. "The life, I think. The arrangement."

"That is a long and complicated story. One I might tell you someday when it won't influence your own decision like it might now," Merritt said. "But what you should know is that we are very happy together. I couldn't imagine my life without both of them. Nor picture how they would be if they were denied each other. It is not what Society might deem normal, whatever that word means. But it is exactly perfect for us."

Vanessa nodded and thought again of the charged moments in the parlor earlier that day. That had felt perfect, too. Like the passion was a circle between them, always flowing round and round. Infinitely exciting and arousing...and comforting.

"And they suggested you three could do something similar?" Merritt asked with a shake of her head. "I might have guessed about Norfolk, but Warwick seems so tightly wound."

"He wasn't earlier today," Vanessa murmured.

Merritt's mouth dropped open. "So you have already agreed and taken part?"

"I did agree, and we did...there was...it was wonderful, Merritt. So passionate and charged and pleasurable. But we didn't...er... complete the...neither of them fully..."

"Fucked you?" Merritt asked mildly. "Be bold about it, my dear. There is nothing better in the world."

Vanessa swallowed. She knew the word. It was sometimes used in the naughty books Merritt shared. It conjured heated, sweaty images now of one or both of these men continuing what they'd started that day.

"Yes," she said. "Other things happened. But not that. They wanted to give me a chance to change my mind now that we...we went so far."

"I see," Merritt said. "So they are tending to your needs first."

Vanessa nodded. "I think so. Though I've made such poor choices in the past, perhaps I do not know how to see the warning signs."

"You've had bad choices thrust upon you by selfish parties," Merritt corrected with a frown. "And beyond an affair, have they spoken at all about your future?"

"Yes. I suppose that is part of their offer. That I might be able to choose between them eventually for a marriage." When Vanessa said it out loud, her heart stuttered.

"I see." Merritt nodded. "That is good, I hoped one of them would step up. Otherwise…well, it doesn't matter."

"Should I do it?" Vanessa asked.

Merritt blinked. "It sounds as though you already have."

"Yes."

"And you enjoyed what happened?"

Vanessa's breath caught. "Very much so. More than anything I've ever experienced before."

"Then what is the harm is going further? In surrendering yourself to pleasure after so long a time fraught with worry and uncertainty and pain?" Merritt caught her hands. "You deserve everything good and more. At worst, it will end in time and you will choose whichever man is a better match for you, thus protecting you from the uncertainty Arthur and your parents have created."

"And at best?"

"You get the life. And the arrangement. And occasionally the library." There was a moment when Merritt's usually strong expression went a little softer with what Vanessa realized was love. Deep and abiding and complete love unlike anything she'd ever seen. What a thing to share that not with just one person, but two. "It's worth it."

Her certainty gave Vanessa more strength and she nodded. "Then I will need even more advice, since you are the far more experienced one in such things. What should I expect, how should I behave?"

"You may expect, I hope, great pleasure from both of them," Merritt said. "The kind of focused, heated, powerful experiences that will change everything about you. But also, if I judge them correctly, you'll get the great joy and arousing pleasure of watching them together."

"They do have...tension between them," Vanessa whispered, and thought of how focused Darrius and Benedict had been when their eyes met, even though they hadn't touched. "The way they look at each other. And it was even more powerful when they were touching me."

"Mmmm," Merritt murmured, and it was clear she was thinking about her own situation. "There is nothing like it."

"And what should I do?" Vanessa asked. "I mean, resting back and letting them sweep me away is all fine and good...more than fine and very good. But at some point I'd like to be a more active participant."

Merritt's gaze lit up further. "Oh, well, *that* I can give advice for! Let us start with the basic seduction of two men..."

Benedict

There had been many long nights in Benedict's life, but none so frustratingly drawn out as the hours between the time he'd shared with Vanessa and Darrius in the parlor and when the house turned in for the night. It was made worse by the fact that the three of them had to pretend away the encounter during supper when all the guests in the house had come together for supper.

There had been so much tension during that meal as the three of them sat with Lord and Lady Egerton and Peter Reid that he was surprised any of them had survived it. But now the clock struck ten, the guests had said their goodnights and he was now standing in the hallway outside of Darrius's door.

Sometimes it felt like he was always waiting in a hallway outside of Darrius's door, and he never knew what would greet him when he entered. Tonight he drew a deep breath and pushed the door open without knocking. The antechamber lamps were lit and the fire glowed. Darrius stood before it, jacket removed, cravat gone, boots discarded and sleeves rolled to his elbows.

Benedict caught his breath. A man could write soliloquies about those forearms. He could spend a lifetime just…touching them.

"You're here," Darrius said softly.

Benedict nodded. "Did you think I wouldn't come?"

"I know you were angry with me in the garden," Darrius said, and for a moment there was vulnerability slashed across his face.

"After wanting you and waiting for you and accepting secrets in the dark from you for so many years, do you think that would keep me away? That anything could?"

Darrius flinched. They never discussed those secrets in the dark. As far as either of them acknowledged they had only ever succumbed to desire once. "Tonight…all of this…it will be about her…not us."

He was repeating his earlier declaration, but there was something in the way his voice broke when he said that, which gave Benedict…hope.

Benedict moved toward him. Darrius tensed, but he didn't back away. He just tracked Benedict's every move, all the way to when he reached out and flattened a palm against Darrius's broad chest. He felt his heartbeat elevate through the thin linen of his shirt.

"Yes, you said that before. Almost like you have to convince yourself. But if I'm near you, it will always be about us," Benedict whispered. "Whether you let me touch you or not."

He edged even closer and Darrius's breath hitched slightly, his blue eyes never leaving Benedict's. He didn't step away when their thighs brushed. He didn't step away when Benedict let his hand slide lower, down Darrius's chest, over his stomach, across his hip.

He leaned in and their lips came perilously close to touching. Darrius turned his head slightly and so Benedict moved those lips across the harsh line of his jaw instead, tasting his skin, wishing he could taste a great deal more of it.

There was a hesitant knock at the door behind them and Darrius made a desperate sound low in his chest. Then he took a long step away and the contact was broken. For a brief second they just stared at each other, the tension between them never higher. Then Darrius stepped away and went to the door.

It was Vanessa, not that Benedict had expected anything different. He'd known she would come. From the first moment he'd seen her watching Merritt with her men, he'd known she would open herself to them.

And he couldn't wait.

She stepped into the room and looked up at Darrius, her brown eyes dilated with desire. They swept over him from head to toe, just as Benedict had looked at him a moment before. And then she swallowed hard.

"Oh. Your arms," she whispered.

Benedict choked on a laugh as he came over to her. "Aren't they beautiful?" he asked, tucking a loose lock of her hair behind her ear. "*He* is extraordinarily beautiful."

Darrius's cheeks flamed slightly. "Benedict."

"He isn't wrong," Vanessa whispered, and her hand fluttered at her side like she wanted to touch him. "I've always thought you… well, I had wrong thoughts about you when you were going to be my brother-in-law."

Darrius seemed surprised by that admission, but not bothered. Oh no, that was something else that glinted in the brightness of the blue. A heat that could burn them all to the ground before they were done, and they would all celebrate it.

Benedict reached back and shut the door firmly, then turned the key in the lock. "I think we've waited long enough, haven't we? If we're going to try this, to give in to what we all clearly want, then let us begin. Through that door." He pointed toward the door that led to the bedchamber. "In his bed."

CHAPTER 8

Vanessa

In the parlor hours before, Vanessa had been taken aback by Benedict and Darrius's shocking offer of pleasure with both of them. She'd been swept away by a fantasy that had taken root and become impossible to walk away from. But in the hours since Benedict had held her on the settee while Darrius made her entire body shake with unbelievable pleasure, she'd had plenty of time to think. To ponder. To weigh options.

And that made this moment when she followed Darrius into his bedchamber, Benedict behind her, his warm hand resting on her back, even more powerful. This was a choice, not a whim. This was reality, not a filmy dream that would fade.

Darrius stepped aside and she looked around her. It was a fine room, likely the one he'd grown up in during his time in the country as a young man. But it fit him now, with its muted colors, stark white linens and big bed. Lord, that was a big bed. It would easily fit them all.

As if it had been made to do so.

Darrius turned and his gaze moved over her in one long sweep.

Then he cleared his throat. "You said that you had wrong thoughts about me when you were going to be my sister-in-law. But before we begin, you need to know that I shared those…forbidden desires." His eyes flitted to Benedict for the briefest of moments and her body clenched. He continued, "I know I said it before, but I meant it."

"And what are you going to do about it?" Benedict asked, his tone low and seductive. "Because she isn't going to be your brother's wife anymore."

Darrius swallowed hard. "I've tasted you, Vanessa. The sweetest, most glorious taste of any woman I've experienced. And I want more of that. I want everything. I want to bury myself so deep inside of you that we don't know where we are separate beings. I want to watch you ride him…" He motioned to Benedict. "…until you are weak. I want you to use me like I was built for nothing but your pleasure."

"Bloody hell," Benedict whispered—whimpered, actually. It was a whimper, filled with longing and need that mirrored her own.

She nodded. "I want all of that. With both of you. And I know a little, thanks to Merritt's…education. But I may need guidance. So tell me where you wish for me to begin."

Darrius reached out and closed lean fingers around her shoulder. He turned her gently to face Benedict and said, "Have her. I want to watch you have her."

This was real and she trembled with anticipation and the power of what would come. With the power of the way Benedict stepped up to her. He slid his fingers into her hair and tilted her mouth to his, then took it.

In the hallway the previous night his kiss had started gentle and then turned hungry, but it was always controlled. This wasn't. His mouth was hard and harsh on her from the start, devouring her like he was starving. She lifted against him with a ragged cry, gripping his lapels with her fists, arching against him without any way to stop it.

"Yes," Darrius whispered, and she felt his fingers on the buttons along the back of her gown. He unfastened them one by one, his fingers dipping in to brush the flesh beneath her silky chemise. The gown fully parted at last and Benedict broke the kiss.

She turned her face toward Darrius without being told to do so and now *he* kissed her, deep and slow and drugging. All the while Benedict tugged her gown, helping her pull it from her arms and then down and over the swell of her hips.

When it pooled at her feet, she kicked it away. Darrius stepped back and the two men stood together, staring at her in her chemise and stockings and slippers. She was embarrassed by being so exposed. She hadn't been so in a very long time and her memories of those encounters were spoiled by the abandonment that had followed.

But when they looked at her, when Darrius licked his lips like she was a sweet he wanted to devour, some of the self-consciousness faded. This was her fantasy, wasn't it? She wasn't going to ruin a moment of it with worry or fear or self-recrimination.

She straightened her spine, arching just a touch before she lifted a hand and lowered the chemise strap from her arm. Then the other. She let it fall away around her feet and she was naked before them.

"Do I please?" she asked, voice trembling.

Benedict didn't answer with words. He caught her around the waist and drew her against him. He cupped her behind the knee, drawing her leg up, grinding against her gently so she felt the hard length of him against her body.

"Very much," he groaned against her lips. "And now it's my turn to please you." He glanced back over his shoulder. "Are you watching?"

"Yes." Darrius's voice was strangled. "I can't look away. Make her shake for me. Make her wet for me."

Already Vanessa moaned, their sensual words playing her like an instrument before either of them had truly touched her in a way that would bring her pleasure. Benedict changed that very quickly. He pushed her toward the bed, lifting her to the edge as he continued to kiss her. Once she didn't have to support her own weight, she wrapped her arms around his neck, drowning in sensation as his kiss deepened.

He pulled away a fraction. "Darrius says you're the sweetest woman he's ever tasted," he whispered. "I want to try."

He didn't wait for her response, but lowered himself down her body, lips just skimming her flesh. She collapsed on her back and lifted her hips, welcoming his mouth. Darrius swore beneath his breath and came to the bed beside her. He kissed her as Benedict widened her legs and burrowed his face between them, sucking and licking as she keened.

She clutched her fingers in his hair, vibrating with the pleasure Benedict created. Like Darrius, he was a virtuoso at playing her body and she edged to the pleasure with every long stroke of his tongue. Darrius bent to her breast and sucked her nipple between his lips, tonguing it like he'd tongued her clitoris earlier in the day. She felt tugged between them, all else fading but the worship of their mouths.

When she came, it was sudden, the pleasure had been building and then it exploded with a rippling power that had her lifting her hips hard against Benedict. He continued to stroke her, just as Darrius had earlier, until the pleasure faded and she went weak. Then he stood and shrugged from his jacket.

"I want you, Vanessa. I want to feel you around me," he said, unwrapping his cravat.

Darrius had still been licking her nipples, but now he stopped and together he and Vanessa stared at the man stripping from his clothing at a rapid pace before them. When he tugged his shirt over his head, they both caught their breath. She turned into Darrius, kissing him, sucking his tongue until he moaned and then turned his face back toward Benedict.

Benedict smiled slightly, as if he realized they wanted the show.

He gave it, removing his boots at a slower pace and then taking his time with the fall front of his trousers. When he let it drop forward and his hard cock curled up around his stomach, she couldn't remember how to breathe.

"Please," she murmured. "Please, please."

He pushed the trousers aside and leaned one hand into the mattress beside her head. The other he pressed to Darrius's thigh, since it was so close to her. She expected the other man to pull away, as he always seemed to do when the tension grew too heavy between them. But he didn't. He let out a soft moan and allowed Benedict to make him his perch as he positioned himself against her entrance. She reached between them and caught him in hand, loving the weight of him, the softness of his skin, the hardness of the length. She stroked him against her and let out a garbled moan when he slid home in one long thrust.

It had been a long time since a man was inside of her. And this man was worlds different than the last. Avebury had taken her quick and hard. Occasionally he touched her, stimulated her as he used her body, and that had brought her pleasure. But the act was for him. She felt it, saw it, tried to pretend it away to no avail.

Benedict was not Avebury. He pushed to the hilt and then he held steady there, exploring her face as if it were the most interesting thing in the world. When he pulsed forward, he ground his hips and she gasped at the ricocheting pleasure that rushed through her sensitive body.

"Oh my God," she gasped, and he smiled.

"That's a good start." He kissed her and there were no more words as he rolled his body against her, grinding and taking, thrusting and pleasuring. She lifted against him, meeting the strokes, crying out as the pleasure mounted.

She looked over to find Darrius watching it all. Benedict followed her gaze and he gasped out, "Touch her."

Darrius started, as if he had forgotten he could be seen in the heat between them. He hesitated a moment, but then he did as he'd been told. He reached between their bodies, he found where they met. And he circled her clitoris with his fingers in time to Benedict's strokes. She came with gasping, grunting cries that echoed in the room. Probably echoed in the house. She didn't care, couldn't care about anything but the soaring heights of her release.

Benedict cursed and then she felt him pull from her, spending against her stomach with long, heavy strokes of his hand. He rolled away and arched a brow at Darrius. A challenge. And one the other man met. Darrius opened his own fall front without removing the rest of his clothing and pushed her legs wide, draping them over his elbows as he stroked into her still clenching sheath.

"Fuck," he grunted, his eyes closing with pure pleasure. "You feel so good."

Benedict made a low sound in his throat, and just as Darrius had done earlier, he reached between them and stimulated her while Darrius began to stroke. She was already on edge from two orgasms, and it took nothing to bring her back to that place. She looked down to where he touched her, where Darrius took her. When Benedict touched her, he also touched Darrius, his fingers playing at the base of the other's man's cock.

She cried out, rolling with the pleasure, with the forbidden desire to see them touch each other even more. With the power of this connection that flowed between them. Darrius fucked her through it, watching her, watching Benedict and moaning out her name when he, too, spent on her stomach. He collapsed over her, his mouth on her throat, his hands in her hair and she tilted her mouth up so Benedict could kiss her before he slid to lie beside them in the quiet of the room where her life had been changed forever.

Darrius

Time had lost all meaning as the three of them lay together in his bed. Had it been moments since they were tangled in each other? Hours? Did it matter? All Darrius could feel was…peace. And he never felt peace. He didn't trust peace.

Vanessa let out a soft sigh and her hand moved to rest on his chest. He was still dressed except for his cock. *They* were naked, Benedict's legs tangled with hers, his hand on her breast where he lightly played. Already, Darrius wanted more. He wanted everything. He wanted to feel Benedict touch him again while Darrius fucked this woman until she screamed.

"Was it too much?" he asked, trying to ground himself in reality.

She lifted her head with a wicked little smile that was so gorgeous on her normally sweet face. "I felt like my moaning might have given you a clue that it was just exactly what I needed." Her fingers stroked his chest through the linen shirt. "You always worry about others, don't you?"

"He does," Benedict said softly.

Darrius let out a small sigh. "I've heard rumors of eldest children who take on that of protector to the rest, but that wasn't my family. Arthur has always been…Arthur. And I've followed behind him, cleaning up his messes, for a very long time. Trying to right his wrongs."

She tensed and Darrius realized he'd made an error. Made her think he meant she was one of those wrongs. And she was…but that hadn't been what he'd been thinking about in the slightest when he touched her, had her.

She lowered her head and refused to look at either of them now. "Is this pity?"

There was a long pause and Darrius sat up a little straighter, forcing her to do the same. "No." He glanced at Benedict and, of course, found him watching him. Benedict was always watching him. Tempting him. Drawing more from him than he felt he could give. He cleared his throat. "When I want something I-I know I can't have…I pull away. I harden myself. I think that's why you saw me as cold toward you. But my desire for you…it is the furthest thing from pity."

He was saying it to her, but he saw those words land with Benedict. Felt them soak through him. Felt them move him.

She sat up and ran a hand through her tangled hair. "I think I should go back to my room. We've given each other a great deal to think about tonight. And look forward to, assuming your offer still stands that we can continue like this."

"For as long as you desire," Benedict said.

"For as long as we're here," Darrius said, a slight correction, but a meaningful one. After all, he couldn't imagine doing this forever. Could he? Or was it just that the image was too powerful?

She slipped from his bed and gathered her things. Benedict helped her dress while Darrius watched them with the same hunger he'd felt when she was being undressed. Their hands moving over each other, her skin against his skin, it was all intoxicating. Bordering on dangerous, because the hunger it unleashed didn't feel controlled, nor did the emotions beneath the surface.

When she was fixed enough to depart, she took a long look at Benedict, still naked, then at Darrius sprawled across his bed, trousers only unfastened, and she smiled slightly. "Thank you for tonight. Thank you for making me feel so…so alive. I didn't realize I was in a tomb until you did that."

She said nothing else, but slipped away, out into the antechamber, away into the hall. Together they stared after her and then Darrius felt Benedict's eyes slide to him. He returned the gaze and shivered at the absolute perfection of this man's naked form.

"Should I go back to my room?" Benedict asked, his tone low and seductive.

Everything in Darrius wanted to say no. To take his hand and draw him in and surrender to every desire that had ever pulsed through his veins. Instead he nodded.

"I think it's best," he said, and wished his voice didn't shake a little.

Benedict gave a half-smile, almost as if he'd expected the answer and won some kind of wager with himself about it. Then he tugged his trousers on and gathered the rest of his things over his arm before he started for the door. There, he turned back.

"Watching you fuck her? It's amazing, Darrius. Gorgeous."

He left and Darrius scrubbed a hand over his face. "Yes," he whispered before he flopped back on the bed and covered his eyes with his forearm.

CHAPTER 9

Vanessa

Although Vanessa had, for most of her adult life, been an early-to-rise sort of person, that was not true the next morning. She had slept so poorly, tormented by memories of her time with the two men and thoughts of the foggy future, that she didn't manage to get up until close to noon. When she got ready with the help of the maid that Darrius had assigned to her and dragged herself downstairs, she found Merritt in the breakfast room, waiting for her.

"At last," the marchioness said as she got to her feet and crossed to her with a knowing smile. "They must have worn you out, my dear."

"Merritt!" Vanessa gasped, and looked toward the door.

She laughed. "Calm yourself. The servants are busy elsewhere and your men seem to be abed still. *Mine* are out for a ride, though I'm not sure what way to take that. I suppose I'll find out when they return by how happy they look."

Vanessa sat down at the table and shook her head. "You are so matter of fact about everything."

"It's time that allows it," Merritt said, and moved to the sideboard to prepare a plate. "To be honest, I'm thrilled to know someone else who is both aware of my relationship with them and also indulges in such a thing herself. I don't have to pretend." She set a plate before Vanessa and smiled. "Now eat. You'll want to keep your strength up. At the beginning, it's all about stamina."

Vanessa picked at her plate a moment, and when Merritt arched a brow at her, she dutifully took a few bites. As she chewed, she stared at her friend. "Yesterday I asked you about the physical aspect of your relationship, but…"

"You wonder about the rest?" Merritt asked.

She nodded. "There's such intensity when we're together, even though we've just begun. It feels like more than physical."

"If you are lucky, it will be. I was happy with Elliot," Merritt said, referring to the marquess by his given name. "We were passionate together, we were well matched when we entered a room. He challenged me and was patient when I needed it. But when he brought Peter back to me…we had loved each other when we were young and been parted when the marriage was arranged…I realized something."

"What was it?" Vanessa asked, leaning forward now. It was impossible not to—Merritt almost glowed with love and certainty and everything Vanessa longed for.

"That I was missing a piece of myself when I didn't have Peter. But more than that, Elliot was missing a piece of himself. In fact, sometimes when I watch them together, I think that he might have needed him even more than I did. Our love for each other, as parts and as a whole, grows with every day we spend together. Whether we're making love or doing something mundane like taking a walk or reading together…it's magic."

Vanessa thought about that for a moment. "I can see how that would be true." She cleared her throat. "I know that you and the gentlemen originally intended to go back to London just after the wedding that never was. I-I think you should do that."

Merritt straightened. "That was before all this happened, my dear. I worry about leaving you to yourself, especially when things are uncertain."

"But not dangerously so, I don't think," Vanessa said. "These men are offering me a chance at a future, as well as a moment in the present that I…I need to explore fully."

"Without friends in the house to keep you from fucking in the gazebo if you'd like to?" Merritt asked.

Vanessa's cheeks heated even as she laughed. "Yes, I suppose so."

Merritt nodded. "I'll tell Elliot and Peter when they return. We can be on the road as early as this evening." She smiled. "Honestly, there is a lovely inn a few hours down the road. We can pretend we just met each other at supper, that there's only one room left and we must share it."

Vanessa shivered at the idea of playing such games with Darrius and Benedict. At becoming so comfortable that erotic moments could be playful as well as powerful.

"Is it good?" Merritt asked, drawing Vanessa back to the present.

It took a moment for her to realize what Merritt was referring to: the passion. The moments in that bed. She jerked her chin down once because there was no other answer, no other feeling. "Oh…oh yes. It was so good. I…I've never been so pleased."

A shadow of a smile crossed Merrrit's lips. "And do the two of them…?"

"No. They danced around the edges, but no further." She frowned. "But the tension between them is remarkable. Oh, Merritt, I want to see it. I want to feel them with each other."

"I hope you can," Merritt said, this time softer, her gaze going distant like she was thinking about her own life. "Encourage them," she suggested. "Let them know that they can trust you, as you are trusting them. That you are excited by their connection."

"I will," Vanessa promised and the idea of doing just that was thrilling.

Merritt got to her feet. "Eat the rest of that. I'll go tell the servants that we'll depart later today."

She squeezed Vanessa's shoulder before she left the breakfast room, left Vanessa to think about what she'd said. And what power she, herself, might wield over two men who seemed to contain so much of it.

～

Benedict

Benedict was frustrated. He'd made plans all night as he tossed and turned in his bed, reliving every moment of the time with Vanessa and Darrius. He'd wanted to find a way to repeat those moments, or some version of them, today. Perhaps slip away together briefly, find some distraction for everyone else so he could…

Well, the possibilities were endless.

Except the best laid plans had been left unrealized. When the Marquess of Egerton and his party had announced that they were departing for London that very day, all attention had shifted to readying them for that sudden change of plans. Darrius had hardly been anywhere to be seen as he took over duties that would have normally been reserved for the viscount. Was that because all those things truly needed to be done so he was forced to take the reins? Or was it about hiding?

Darrius was expert at both, and so it was hard to know.

As for Vanessa, she'd been spending a great deal of time with the marchioness, helping her ready for the trip and organizing food to be packed for the road. In truth, she was acting as viscountess might.

Would she choose a life with Darrius at the end of this affair? The two of them stepping into roles of responsibility even when they weren't official. They would be well-matched if they did. Good partners.

So why did the idea make his stomach hurt a little?

He turned from the window in the parlor where he'd been nursing his disappointment and went into the foyer. As if conjured by his thoughts, Vanessa came down the stairs at just that moment, walking with the butler and giving him some instruction.

"Thank you, Turner," she said with a smile. An expression that fluttered when she glanced over and found Benedict standing in the parlor door.

He couldn't resist her then. He caught her hand and drew her down the dim hallway. No one was around, and he could wait any longer. He pressed her against the wall and leaned in, taking her mouth with the hunger he had been suppressing since she left the bed last night.

She seemed stunned for a moment, but then she let out a low gasp into his mouth and wound her arms around his neck. She returned his kiss with fervor, lifting against him gently, as if seeking pleasure he certainly couldn't give when they were in a public area, the house buzzing with activity.

Or he could, but there might be consequences.

He pulled back a fraction and smiled down at her. "I have been wanting to do that for hours and hours."

She was breathless. "I'm glad you did."

There was the clearing of a throat behind them and they both turned. Darrius had exited the study and was staring at them. Benedict almost laughed. No wonder Vanessa had mistaken the other man's desire for dislike. His expression was hard in the glint of lamplight, but Benedict knew he was aroused by what he saw. It was in the ripple of the muscle in his jaw, in the way his fingers flexed at his side.

Benedict held his stare, lost in blue fire for a moment. Then he turned Vanessa toward him and nudged her forward even while he kept his front pressed to her back. "Do you want to kiss her, too?"

Darrius sucked in a breath, the only sound in the quiet. Then he nodded. Benedict slid a hand along her throat to tilt her face upward toward him. Darrius caught her with a growl and kissed her. When he moved to cup her cheek, his fingers slid across Benedict's and now it was Benedict who lost his breath.

Vanessa's fingers clenched against Darrius's jacket as their kiss deepened and filled with the promise of passion to come. And come and come and come, Benedict hoped. There was something magical about having her pressed between them, her movements teasing both of them. He wanted to have her this way, both of them buried in her body, their cocks separated by nothing but a thin membrane of flesh.

He was almost dizzy with the image as Darrius finally pulled away from her and stepped back, his breath short and his gaze a little unsteady. "The sooner we say our goodbyes, the sooner we get to continue that," he said, his voice rough and laced with the same desire that coursed through Benedict's veins.

It was so powerful to see it. Darrius held back so much, denying himself pleasure and even emotion. But with Vanessa...well, she brought him out of that protective shell a little. Made him more of the man Benedict had always believed he could be. That he longed for him to be.

"I agree," Vanessa said, and smoothed her gown with both hands. She smiled back over her shoulder at Benedict. "And I hear the Egerton party coming down now, so it seems the time has come. Shall we, gentlemen?"

Benedict arched a brow at Darrius, who was also smiling at how she took charge. "After you," Darrius said with a great flourish to motion her back toward the foyer.

Benedict followed and they found Lord and Lady Egerton and Reid standing together. They all looked a little...flushed, and Benedict almost laughed. Seemed they weren't the only threesome who'd been up to a bit of naughty mischief before departure.

Egerton stepped forward and extended a hand to Darrius. "You're handling this mess like a true gentleman, Warwick."

Darrius glanced briefly at Vanessa, but then nodded. "Thank you, Egerton."

The men continued to shake hands even as Lady Egerton enfolded Vanessa in a hug. "When you return to London, come see me," she said. "Whatever happens, we will work together on the next steps." She glanced at Benedict meaningfully and then at Darrius as she released Vanessa.

"And in the meantime, we will do what we can in London," Reid said.

Egerton nodded. "I will have a stern meeting with your parents, Vanessa. They will cause you no trouble either way. And if I find Arthur Warwick…"

He trailed off and inclined his head at Darrius, as if asking him what he desired. Darrius folded his arms. "Please feel free to punch my brother in the mouth if you find him. On my behalf."

That elicited a rare smile from the marquess, and Benedict couldn't help but notice how very handsome the man was. No wonder the marchioness and Reid were so obsessed with him.

"I shall do that and pass along your regards." He placed a hand on Merritt's back and guided her toward the door. "Come along then, you two."

They loaded into the carriage, made their final waves of goodbye and then they were off, racing down the drive. And finally, Benedict was alone with the two people he couldn't resist.

He turned, smiling at them both, and said, "Finally. And now may I suggest we retire back to Darrius's room? Because there's nothing I'd like more than to continue what we started in the hall-way. With far fewer layers of clothing, of course."

Darrius took Vanessa's hand and tugged her gently toward the house. "I thought you'd never ask.

Vanessa

As the three of them staggered upstairs and down the hallway toward Darrius's chamber, the energy had been light. Playful even. But the moment the chamber door closed and locked, that shifted. Darrius spun her into his arms and his mouth was hot on hers like it had been in the hallway, his fingers dragging into her hair, gripping her scalp to turn her head and deepen the passionate kiss. Benedict didn't hesitate either—he was at her back, grinding against her. The feel of them flanking her, pressing her between them, was almost overwhelming in its pleasure.

She reached back, cupping Benedict's cheek, and he leaned in as Darrius pulled back, the two men almost brushing lips in the exchange. She would have asked them to, but Benedict silenced her with his mouth. Her dress was being removed. She had no idea which one of them was doing it. It was just hands now, just fingers brushing her, pulling fabric down, sliding against her skin as she moaned in pleasure and anticipation.

The dress was tossed aside and as Benedict continued to kiss her, Darrius dropped to his knees before her and untied her garters. His mouth dragged along the line of the top of her stocking and she shuddered with the sensation. He rolled the silky stockings down, unbuckled her slippers. His hands were hot on her bare skin as he retraced the line back up her leg and repeated the action on the other side.

His fingers slid higher now, brushing between her legs, urging her to open to him. She couldn't resist. She was already too swept away, there was no going back. She widened her stance, granting him some access and broke away from Benedict's kiss. They both stared down at Darrius, this powerful man on his knees for her and she realized that the way Benedict was standing, it would be so easy for Darrius to lick him, too.

And once again her fantasies were stoked. A fire that exploded further when Benedict pushed her hair back over her shoulder and kissed the sensitive spot where her shoulder and neck met.

She felt like she was in suspension as she waited for Darrius to lick her, but he continued to watch her with Benedict for a moment before he asked, "Have you ever had a man in your mouth?"

CHAPTER 10

Vanessa

The question hung in the air, held captive by the tension that image created between them. Slowly she shook her head. "I-I've seen illustrations. But never tried it."

Darrius didn't respond for a moment. His gaze remained on her face, even as he finally did as she'd been waiting for and stroked his tongue between her legs. His eyes shifted toward Benedict and he stared at the obvious cockstand so close to his face. He pulled away and she shivered at the loss of his touch. "Suck him," he said.

She reached down to trace Benedict's hard cock with her hand. "I don't know how."

"I'll help you," Darrius said as he pushed to his feet.

She nodded, enthralled by that idea, equally enthralled by the way Benedict moaned at the image. "But I want you both to undress. It's unfair otherwise."

Darrius laughed a little and went to work on his clothing. Benedict did the same and soon they were both naked. She stared. Every other time they'd done this, she'd been so swept away, so overcome.

But everything had slowed now. They had time, there would be no interruptions. It was only this and them.

So she could stare to her heart's content. They were very different men. Benedict was lanky, tall and narrow hipped. His cock was longer and when he stoked it, it got longer still. Darrius had broad shoulders, thick thighs...good God, those thighs, and a curling line of hair that directed one to the equally thick cock between his legs.

Her hands shook as she stepped forward and took each of them in hand, feeling the heat of them, the length, the hardness. It seemed to surprise them that she'd been so bold, because they let out a tandem moan, even as they watched her stroke them side by side.

Exciting them was everything. Seeing the reactions when she increased or decreased her pace, the intensity of her grip. But at last, they seemed to make a silent agreement that playtime was over. Darrius motioned Benedict to lean on the edge of the bed as Darrius kissed her. Hard and fast and heated.

Then he turned her around roughly and helped her bend at the waist toward Benedict. She braced one hand beside his hip and took him in hand with the other.

"Lick him," Darrius said, a little breathless. "Just taste him."

She did as she'd been ordered, watching Benedict's face as she traced her tongue over his length from the base to the tip. His hands gripped the mattress edge and he moaned. "Christ."

She felt Darrius's fingers move into her hair. "Close your mouth around him and suck him. No teeth."

She gripped the base of Benedict's cock and once again followed Darrius's order. She closed her lips around him, slowly taking him into her mouth until she felt she could take no more. She sucked gently, testing him with her tongue.

"Now pump," Darrius whispered, his voice shaky as he started to gently guide her head up and down. She surrendered to the pleasure of this act, watching as Benedict's eyes came shut for a moment, as his shoulder strained with the pleasure and the control exerted so he wouldn't touch her. When he opened those same dark eyes, he wasn't watching her, he was watching Darrius. She was the conduit between them, she realized. Darrius's proxy in making this man his.

And that excited her even more. She took Benedict deeper, swirling her tongue around his length as he hissed a gasp of pleasure.

"Look at him," Darrius gasped. "Watch her."

They met eyes at his commands and her heart throbbed. God, but these men were powerful. She loved pleasing and being pleased by them. And in that moment, she felt Darrius's cock rubbing against her sex.

She moaned around Benedict's cock and he swore as he pushed his hand into her hair, his fingers tangling with Darrius's right in the moment that he took her in one long thrust. She sucked Benedict harder in response, her moans buried against his length.

The rest of the world was forgotten as she ground back against Darrius and stroked her mouth over Benedict. It was all sensation, tingling pleasure that seemed to surround her from all sides. As he took her faster, Darrius guided her head against Benedict, helping her find a rhythm that had him arching and moaning and crying out her name in the quiet. His legs began to shake, his hands gripping her hair and Darrius's fingers and the edge of the mattress. And then he moaned and pushed her aside as he came.

No sooner had he done that than he leaned in and caught her lips, kissing her deeply. His fingers slid down the apex of her body and he stroked her clitoris as Darrius fucked her harder and faster and with increasing urgency, like he was on the edge of the control. So was she, and a few flicks of Benedict's expert fingers had her convulsing around Darrius's cock, waves of pleasure taking her and sweeping her away until she was collapsed in Benedict's arms and she felt Darrius spend across her back.

Benedict lifted her, shifting her onto the bed beside him, Darrius on her other side. They lay like that for a little while, panting breaths eventually slowing and matching. Darrius stroked one of her breasts absently while Benedict did the same with the other. Their hands were so close and when she looked up at them she saw Darrius was watching Benedict, his blue eyes stormy with continued desire. Benedict stared at Darrius's hand, like he was fascinated by the movement of his fingers. She thought of what Merritt had told her before she left.

"Touch him," she whispered, nudging Darrius gently.

He jerked his gaze from Benedict's face to hers and she saw all his worry and fear and pain and regret flash there in an instant so powerful it nearly stole her breath. She leaned up and kissed his jawline gently. "Touch him, Darrius. Please."

∼

Darrius

All Darrius wanted to do was surrender to exactly what Vanessa ordered him to do. But he hesitated, pulled back by the same currents that always stole him from whatever desire he felt for Benedict.

"He won't," Benedict said softly, his tone rough and low as he speared Darrius with a challenging look. "He doesn't want you to see."

She was breathless when she asked, "See what?"

"Anything," Benedict said.

Darrius shut his eyes. His body was still reeling from the power of what he'd shared with these two, it felt impossible to come up with the arguments it felt like he needed. "That's—that's not fair," he managed.

Benedict arched a brow. "I agree."

Vanessa was watching them back and forth as the arguments that always sat beneath the surface bubbled to the forefront. She placed a hand on Darrius's bare arm, a calming element in the midst of a storm he'd been fighting for so long.

"Have you been together before?" she asked, just as gently.

He looked down at her, but he saw no censor, no judgment. None of the things he feared when he pictured truly surrendering himself this way. And she had asked Darrius to touch Benedict, hadn't she? He drew a shallow breath and looked at Benedict.

"Yes," he admitted, the first time he'd said it out loud to any other person.

Her lips parted. "More than once?"

Benedict nodded. "Yes. Although perhaps he would only admit the one time."

Darrius flopped back on the bed with a curse. But it didn't stop Vanessa from shaking her head and pressing forward. "What...what does that mean, Darrius?"

He clutched the coverlet with his fists, as if the feel of the fabric could center him. It didn't. Nothing could now. He was spiraling toward an end he'd always known would come. From the first moment he met Benedict Norfolk in school and felt the powerful, passionate draw to him that had never left. Even when he tried to force it away. Ignore it away.

"Two years ago we had an...encounter...after a night of drinking in London," he admitted softly.

"And since then?" Benedict encouraged.

Darrius glared at him. "If you want to tell it so badly, then you do it."

Benedict broke their stare and looked at her instead. "Since then, there have been a handful more encounters. But always at clubs for gentlemen of...certain desires. Always masked. Always anonymous where he can pretend he isn't him and I'm not me. Where I can be a meaningless cock in the dark that he sucks. We've never discussed it."

"Until now," Darrius said. "We're discussing it now."

"Why do you...hide like that?" she asked. "Is it only Society's judgment or something more?"

Darrius hesitated. To tell her that was to open a door he might never be able to close. It would tell her more about him than he felt comfortable sharing with anyone. Even her. Even him. At some point he would have to, he thought. If marriage to her was on the table, she would need to know his…limitations. Especially when the way she touched him made him long for more.

But right now, he didn't want to do that.

It was like she saw it. Her expression softened and she rolled to half cover him. She cupped his cheeks and kissed him gently, almost like she was offering balm on a wound he kept pretending didn't exist. When she drew back, she pushed from his bed.

"Let me see," she whispered. "If I cannot hide from you, I don't want you to hide from me. Please, Darrius, let me see."

His lips parted and he shifted his stare to Benedict. But of course he wouldn't offer sanity in the midst of this madness. When it came to desire, Benedict always demanded more. And now his expression pleaded as much as hers.

"Please, Darrius," he said, repeating her words as he edged closer.

Darrius shivered as Benedict cupped his cheek. He didn't turn away when he leaned in. He didn't stop him when he bent his head and did the one thing Darrius had wanted and always denied himself.

Benedict kissed him.

Darrius had been avoiding just this thing for years because he'd pictured how powerful it would be. And he hadn't been wrong. Benedict took his lips, drove his tongue past them to war with his, and it was…everything. Everything he'd dreamed, everything he'd wanted, everything he'd feared in the dark of night when all he could think about was this man. He was carried away by it, by the passion of the kiss and the emotions that roared to the surface of his mind and body and soul.

He couldn't pull away, so he didn't. He hauled Benedict over him, holding him tighter, tasting every inch of his mouth as Benedict arched against him and moaned his name like he was drowning. At least they would sink together.

Benedict pulled back, staring down into Darrius's face, like he was seeing him for the first time. Then he smiled. "I've wanted to do that for so long." He leaned back down and kissed him more gently. "So fucking long."

Darrius lifted against him, relief and love flowing through him. Love for this man that terrified him. He pushed it away and focused instead on the feel of Benedict's hand gliding down his side, nails raking gently along his ribs so that he shivered.

Benedict pulled back from the kiss. "You did such a good job with your mouth, Vanessa," he whispered.

Darrius followed his stare. Vanessa was still standing by the bed, eyes shining with desire as she watched them.

"But," Benedict continued, "I want to show you a little more. If you'll let me."

Darrius moaned. Every time he and Benedict had come smashing together, masked and pretending, he had been the one to take Benedict in his mouth. So he wouldn't lose control. But now he couldn't hold back anymore. This was happening and he wanted to enjoy every moment.

"Yes," he moaned. "Please."

Benedict smiled again, so beautiful, and then he slid his mouth down Darrius's neck, across his chest, over his stomach. He caught him in hand, hard again despite the recent release, and stroked him while he traced the line of his hip with his tongue. Darrius moaned harshly at the spiking pleasure through his cock. Doubled when Benedict covered him with his mouth and began to stroke all the way to the back of his throat.

Vanessa edged closer, studying the way Benedict's mouth moved, the way his hand gripped. She threaded her fingers through Darrius's clenching hand, but she kept watching. Smiling when Darrius couldn't hold back the sounds that were the song of his pleasure.

Benedict brought him all the way to the edge of release, teasing him there, making him ache because he knew a few more strokes, sucks would take him over the edge. But instead Benedict drew back, his dark eyes glinting.

"I want to fuck you," he whispered. "I want to take you."

Darrius couldn't control the full-body shiver at that idea. Of being claimed by this man in a manner that they couldn't pretend away. He nodded, still pulled out to sea by the pleasure. Slowly he rolled over. He crooked his finger toward Vanessa, and when she came, he tugged her onto the bed. They shifted, moving together to find a place. She slid beneath him, opening her legs to him, never resisting when he aligned himself to her body.

He didn't take her yet, though. No, not yet. He waited as Benedict moved around behind him, opening drawers, trying to find something to ease the way.

"There's a small bottle of oil by my bed," Darrius choked out as Vanessa leaned up and began to lick and suck his neck. He felt so sensitive that his cock throbbed in time to her touch.

Benedict gave a low chuckle as he found what he was looking for and returned. He positioned himself on his knees behind Darrius, settling his hands on his hips. "My God, but you are something," he murmured. He leaned around Darrius's shoulder and looked at Vanessa. "We're going to take his control, Vanessa. We're going to make him forget everything but us and this."

"Yes," she groaned. "Oh yes, yes, yes. I want to."

She cupped Darrius's cheeks and pulled him down to kiss her. As she did, Benedict began to work at Darrius's arse with fingers slick with the warm oil. Darrius grunted, thrusting just the head of his cock into Vanessa's clenching sheath as pleasure bombarded from both where he was taking and where he was being readied. He had never had this pleasure, avoided it except in his most heated dreams. But now that it was happening, it was heady and sweet and powerful.

Benedict moaned as he stretched Darrius's arse, gentle as he worked him. And finally, Darrius felt the head of his cock there, pressing gently. Darrius pushed back a little, taking it further, loving the pleasure-pain mixture of the act. Benedict cried out and then he thrust harder, past resistance. When he did so, he forced Darrius forward and he, too, filled Vanessa to the hilt.

They lay there for a moment, Benedict buried in Darrius, Darrius buried in Vanessa. It was a flood of sensation rolling through Darrius's body, so much pleasure that he wanted to spend right then and there. Benedict began to move and Vanessa lifted. Together they worked at Darrius, their hands moving over him, their bodies gripping and taking his in tandem. He moaned and cried out, throwing his head back as he rode the waves they created that were just for him. He was their center, required to give nothing but his pleasure.

And he did, rolling with the sensation, gripping Vanessa's hips as he took her, reveling in the heat of Benedict's breath on his shoulder. And then the nip of his teeth as he rode harder. Vanessa had begun to touch herself as they moved together, and he watched her face as she strained and arched beneath him, as wild with this as he was.

When she came, her pussy gripped him, powerful waves of pleasure that milked his own rising need. Benedict was wild behind him, grunting as he took and it was all too much. Darrius cried out and he poured into Vanessa's body with a roar that matched Benedict's as he did the same, pouring his release into Darrius.

They collapsed into a pile together, sweaty arms and legs, come streaked along their thighs, mouths finding each other as they came down from the most powerful high Darrius had ever experienced.

And he never wanted this dream to end.

Vanessa

After the powerful explosion of desire and passion that had happened in Darrius's bed, Vanessa had readied herself for the consequences. And yet, none had come as of yet. They had separated eventually, each going to their own quarters to bathe and rest and ready for supper. And think about what had happened, she supposed.

Merritt hadn't been wrong when she said watching two men together could be powerful. It had been one of the most glorious experiences of Vanessa's life, to see Benedict and Darrius move as one. To feel their restrained passion finally come loose so they could give and take to and from each other with an abandon that felt animal and wild.

It was tempered now as they sat at the supper table together. Darrius was at the head, Benedict at one hand, she at the other. Rather like in the bed earlier when he had been the center of their focus.

And now he was…calm. Relaxed, even. She didn't think she'd ever seen him this way before. But his normally unreadable expression was eased, he even smiled from time to time, almost always when it came to something Benedict said.

She leaned on her elbow and looked at him more closely, eliciting one of those swift smiles, herself. "And what is that look, Vanessa?" he asked.

"You are very different from Arthur," she murmured.

He froze in the act of cutting his food and the ease vanished from his expression as his lips pursed. "I certainly hope so."

She probably should have stopped pushing then. Stopped driving. But she didn't want to. She wanted to know this man, really understand him. Benedict would let her in, she felt it, she *knew* it. Some part of her was already lost to it and to the comfort he provided by just smiling at her. But Darrius needed prodding. His regard had to be earned and driven.

"Why?" she asked. "How did you manage to be so separate a person from your brother?"

He set his fork down and stared at the plate. She shifted her gaze to Benedict, who had also set his cutlery down. He held her stare in encouragement for a moment, strength pulsing between them. It helped her when she wanted to take back her question.

"My…my father was reckless," Darrius said at last. "He gambled and whored around. My mother was little better. Once she bore my father sons, she was off in the countryside, creating scandals he had to pay to hide. And my brother is, as you know better than anyone, equally imprudent. I saw all three of them destroy worlds with their irresponsibility. And I swore that I would be…better. Be in control."

She glanced at Benedict. "You knew them for a long time. You saw this?"

"Yes." His voice was a little shaky. "Even at school I saw how Arthur reveled in the messes he created, while Darrius followed behind, trying to clean it all up."

"And you made attempts to help me, if I recall. You paid off some of his debts, even." Darrius bent his head. "When I failed to do so."

"It wasn't either of your responsibilities," Vanessa said softly, hating the pain that laced Darrius's every word.

"And yet the results still fall on my head."

"That's why…" Vanessa hesitated and looked again at Benedict. She thought of what they'd told her earlier, about the passion Darrius kept restrained, only unleashing it when he was supposedly anonymous. "That's why you never lean into what you want."

Darrius pursed his lips. "I share their blood, don't I? That means I share their weaknesses. I mean, think about today. I was…irresponsible the last time we were together."

"Are you talking about when you spent in me?" she asked.

He nodded and worry lined his expression again. "I would not ever do something that would trap or harm you. And yet I did."

She shook her head. "I am not during a time in my courses where a pregnancy is very likely."

"Even if it were, we are talking about one of us marrying her at the end. So a baby, while not planned, wouldn't be the worst outcome," Benedict said softly.

Darrius looked a little relieved that he hadn't found censure. But he still sighed. "Still, if I let go like that or in other ways…I might spiral into their failures."

"You never could!" Benedict said, his tone harsh now, hollow. It pained him to see Darrius's pain. What a gift he was to this man… to her.

Still, she didn't react outwardly to that, but took Darrius's hand, lifting it to her lips to kiss his knuckles. She felt the ripple effect of that gesture in his shifting posture. He met her gaze, that pure blue drawing her in and holding her there. Taking her breath. Moving her heart. "That you are letting go now for me…for us…thank you, Darrius."

He seemed surprised by her statement. And more surprised when she released him and went back to her supper with a purposefully bright smile. "Now, I have to ask, when you were last in London, did either of you go to the Royal Theatre?"

Benedict looked as confused as Darrius did at the change of subject, but he answered in the affirmative and they began a far more benign conversation about art and theatre and anything other than their charged affair. Or their fears.

It wasn't that she didn't want to know more about who Darrius was. Or comfort him as he made these difficult confessions. It was that if she pushed him too far, she could see he would shove her away the same way he had done over and over with Benedict. She had to learn from that fact and go slowly. Open the door, then show him it could be shut again when he desired it. Ask him for trust and reward it with relief from the painful subjects his faith revealed.

She didn't think Benedict could do that. She could see that he'd been frustrated for years in his push and pull with Darrius. It brought up his own fears. *She* had to be more delicate. And hope that she could create a place where all three of them might find safety and hope.

Because she had seen into Darrius in these brief moments. And she was enthralled with him, enthralled with Benedict. She didn't want to lose either of them and she had to hope there would be a way that she wouldn't.

<h1 style="text-align:center">CHAPTER 11</h1>

Darrius

In the years since Darrius had privately acknowledged his desire for Benedict, since he'd realized the other man felt the same need, he'd allowed himself fantasies. Not many, because dreams of what might be had felt so dangerous. But occasionally, when his mind was loosened by drink, he'd lain in his bed and let himself imagine a life where he and Benedict could be together.

It was nothing compared to the last few days in the reality of exactly that. He and Benedict making love to Vanessa, to each other. Their threesome becoming closer as they ate and laughed and talked. It was all passion and surrender with them both. And his attachment to each of them and to what they shared as a group, grew with each passing moment.

Sometimes he woke in the night and found Benedict's hand on his stomach, Vanessa's hair fanned out on his chest, and he felt... content.

It was such an unfamiliar feeling, but there it was.

He glanced across the terrace where he was sitting and found

Vanessa and Benedict standing together. She was leaning on the terrace wall, pointing out across the garden at something she saw. Benedict smiled, and even from a distance there was no denying the indulgent adoration on his face. He said something and she laughed, straightening up and lightly swatting him.

It was so easy with them. Their bond grew quickly and powerfully as their affair drew on. But it would end soon, it had to when they returned to London in a few days' time. And then she would have to choose. Wouldn't she choose Benedict? It was obvious they cared deeply for each other. Couldn't they be happy?

And did he love them enough to let them be? To let them go?

"I beg your pardon, sir," Turner said as he came onto the terrace.

Darrius turned his head and blocked the sun with a hand. "What is it, Turner?"

"You have a guest."

Darrius blinked. "A guest? Who?"

"Me." The Marquess of Egerton stepped around Turner, ignoring the butler's pointed look at his intrusion beyond protocol. The handsome man's lips were tight and he looked at Darrius with…God, was that pity?

Darrius got to his feet. "It's fine, Turner. Leave us."

"Egerton!" Vanessa called out, and she and Benedict swiftly came across the terrace to them. "What are you doing here? Are Merritt and Peter here, as well?"

She looked so exuberant that Darrius's stomach turned. He knew for certain that this man was here with no good news. "What has happened?" he asked.

"I'm so sorry," Egerton said, and there was genuine regret to his deep voice. "I came as soon as I could so you would receive this news from…from a friend. I…your brother, Warwick. Arthur is dead."

Benedict

Those horrible words slammed into Benedict's chest like a man twice his size had pressed his hands there and shoved, but somehow he maintained his balance and instead stepped forward. It was good that he did, because Darrius wobbled beneath each syllable's weight. Benedict caught his elbow before he collapsed to his knees, shoring him up as best he could. When Darrius stared up at him, the heartbreak and pain in his eyes nearly killed Benedict. Because he would do anything to protect this man from pain.

"No," Darrius breathed at last. His voice broke. "No, that cannot be true. Arthur cannot be dead, Egerton. You must be mistaken."

Egerton ran a hand through his hair. "Why don't we sit? I can explain."

"Yes," Vanessa said, pale as paper even as she motioned to one of the chairs at the table. "Please tell us."

Benedict helped Darrius back to his place and sat beside him. He didn't give a damn what anyone thought at that moment, so he drew Darrius's hand into his lap, holding tight to him and happy that he was allowed that, probably because the shock of this news kept his lover from second guessing himself.

Vanessa sat beside Egerton, her dark eyes teary with emotion. The marquess shifted as if this was all very uncomfortable. "When we arrived back in London, we immediately began searching for Lord Warwick, as we had discussed. Peter and I put all our joint resources into the matter. We were close to uncovering his whereabouts when the word came." Egerton shook his head. "He'd been racing in a park. Your maid was with him, Vanessa. It was for money, I have heard, though there are few details from those involved. They were going too fast and they…they lost control. Both of them were killed instantly."

Darrius slumped, all color leaving his face as he stared into nothingness. Benedict held his hand all the tighter.

"Going too fast," Darrius whispered. "How fitting."

"Oh, poor Arthur," Vanessa said. "And poor Mary."

Benedict looked at her and felt a swell of adoration for her. This woman had been hurt and humiliated by both these people and yet she still retained some kindness for them.

"Peter and Merritt have been taking care of as much as they can in your stead," Egerton said. "And you know the marchioness—she has cut down anyone who dared breathe of scandal about either Arthur's truncated wedding or his tragic demise."

"I very much appreciate that," Darrius grunted. "As much good as it will do."

"Darrius," Vanessa said, reaching over to set her hand on his and Benedict's interlocked fingers. "My love, I'm so very sorry. For both of you."

Darrius looked at her and then Benedict. He reached out and touched Benedict's face, clearly not caring what Egerton saw in the moment. "Oh, Benedict. You two were such good friends."

It allowed Benedict to feel a slash of the pain he knew would eventually overcome him. But he pushed it back for now. Darrius needed him. The rest would wait. The grief would be there and they would share it, or at least he hoped they would and that Darrius wouldn't use it as a reason to push away. Walk away.

"We must go to London," Darrius said, pulling his hand free as if to accentuate Benedict's fear. "Immediately."

"Of course, you are correct," Vanessa said, and she squeezed Benedict's hand as if to comfort him about Darrius pulling away.

Benedict stood and smoothed his jacket. In this moment, all he could do was help Darrius get to Town where he would have a great deal to do and manage. "Yes," he said. "I will make all the arrangements."

"I'll help you," Egerton said as he followed Benedict into the house. He looked out the window as they left the room in time to see Vanessa come to Darrius, wrapping her arms around his waist from behind.

And to see Darrius bend his head at her support. At least he would allow that. For a little while.

CHAPTER 12

Vanessa

The trip back to London had been a blur. Benedict and Darrius had ridden on horseback to get there as fast as possible, leaving her to ride in the carriage with Egerton. The marquess had been kind. He hadn't pried. He'd even read to her from a favorite book and chatted with her about meaningless subjects to keep her mind from wandering.

It meant nothing. All she'd been able to think about was the two men she loved.

Because she did love them. Both of them. It had not hit her like a thunderbolt, but just settled in her heart like it had always been there. And perhaps it had, this love, just waiting for the right two who could make her life better.

It should have brought her joy to have found them. But she couldn't feel it. She'd been staying with Merritt for the few days she'd been back in London. Benedict called every day, looking haggard and exhausted and emotional. She held him, as warmed by his presence as she hoped she warmed him. She asked about Darrius and felt so helpless that she wanted to scream. Darrius she had not seen since their sudden departure from the countryside. She waited for him even now and hoped today he would bring her other love with him at last.

"Mr. Norfolk to see you, Miss Gardner," Merritt's butler said, and stepped aside to let Benedict enter the parlor where she had been lost in thought.

She jumped to her feet as he pushed the door shut behind himself and crossed to her. He was alone again and her heart sank. Still, she pulled him in, breathing in his scent, holding him close to her until he let out his breath in a long sigh like he'd been holding it in.

"The only pleasure I have is seeing you every day," he said, and allowed her to lead him to the settee.

"How are you, my love?" she asked.

He smiled at the endearment, one she used with him whenever she saw him. They had not declared their feelings, but she refused to hide them. "I'm...tired. And now that we're resolving more and more around Arthur's death, I feel the loss of my friend keenly. I hope that doesn't hurt you to hear, considering your history with him."

"He was clearly a complicated person. I knew him very little, after all. But in some ways, I think it must be harder when the loss is of a person you felt anger toward. I begrudge neither you or Darrius your pain I'm only sorry you must endure it." She sighed. "And how is...*he?*"

They didn't clarify the *he*. Benedict bent his head. "*He* allows me to help, at least. Gives me chores to lighten his load. But..."

"Nothing else," she whispered, heart sinking.

"No. He is isolating himself from me, just as he did after the first time we connected physically all those years ago. Building walls that feel more insurmountable than ever." He scrubbed a hand over his face. "Now that he is viscount, it will be worse."

She winced. The title had fallen to Darrius the moment Arthur breathed his last. And while he would be a far greater steward to the title handed down to him, she feared Benedict was correct. Darrius would shoulder all the weight of responsibility and convince himself even more than there was no room for him to feel anything wild or free or dangerous.

They sat together quietly for a moment, simply holding hands. Benedict was trying to put on a good face for her benefit, but she could read him too well now. She reached out and stroked his cheek with her fingers. "Do you love him?" she asked.

She knew the answer. She needed to hear it.

His breath became wobbly and his eyes misted with unshed tears. "I have loved Darrius Warwick for longer than I haven't," he murmured. "For as long as I have known him, probably. I kept my friendship with poor Arthur long after I would have ended it, just to be nearer to Darrius, to be honest. But...I don't think he'll ever let himself love *me*."

The pain of that statement tore at her, but for the first time in perhaps her whole life, her strength overpowered her anguish. These men had offered her strength when she felt broken. She would find strength to give back to them, to fight because they were too weary.

She cupped his cheeks. "I love him, too," she admitted. "I ache for him. And I ache for you and love you, Benedict Norfolk."

He caught his breath. "Vanessa..."

She smiled. "I don't want to lose either of you. I don't want to choose between you. I don't want any of us to have to sacrifice. And I won't let him put himself in a lonely tower just because he fears his heart."

His breath hitched. "What are you saying?"

"That we'll go to him. Right now. And have this out once and for all."

Benedict slumped a little. "I don't know, Vanessa. I fear I will break if he pushes me away again."

"You won't," she declared, her certainty growing with each word. "Because I won't let him do that to either of us."

He stared at her and then a shadow of his usual bright smile cascaded over his face. He kissed her then, soft at first, then with more purpose. She clung to his wrists with a sigh and sank into the sensation. The one she would not surrender.

"I love you, too, you know," he whispered against her lips.

And she had known it. This feeling had been swift and unexpected and powerful, but it was true. It was real. She drew back. "Then you'll trust me."

He nodded. "With all my heart. And his."

She could only hope she would be worthy stewards of both. And win the war she feared was about to come.

Darrius

It was a funny thing to hate a desk. But as Darrius sat at the desk in his brother's...no, *his* townhouse, he did despise it. It was the desk of the viscount, the study of the viscount. It had been his layabout grandfather's and his cheating father's and his grasping brother's. And now it fell to him and it felt like a weight around his neck, just as the rest of the duties did. Just as the grief did.

"A caller, my lord," said the servant who lightly tapped at his door, a black armband around his bicep.

Darrius rubbed his eyes. "More creditors?"

"No, sir. Mr. Norfolk and Miss Gardner."

He jerked his head up. Benedict had come every day since their return, quietly taking duties from his desk when they became overwhelming, offering gentle advice and quiet support. Darrius knew he'd pushed him away with his gruffness. But yet he was here. And so was Vanessa. Vanessa, who he dreamed of every night and longed for every day.

"Let Norfolk bring her," he said. "And do not disturb us."

The servant inclined his head and slipped away. Darrius knew he only had a few moments to compose himself. It wasn't that big of a house. He got to his feet and smoothed his jacket reflexively. And when the door to the study opened, he forgot everything but the two people who walked in.

Vanessa wore a dark blue gown that brought out the warmth of her cheeks and the beauty of her eyes. Eyes that met his with kindness and hope and all the welcome he could ever desire in this cold world. Benedict had her arm but when he saw Darrius, his gaze moved over him in a long sweep.

"Darrius," Vanessa said softly, and she came to him in a few long strides.

He should have backed away, but he couldn't. Instead, he rested his forehead on her shoulder as her arms came around him, hands smoothing his back. There was peace here, in this woman's embrace. And he breathed her in for a moment before he remembered himself.

"I can't," he whispered, and turned away, going back behind the desk as if the barrier could protect him.

"Why?" she asked. There was no judgment in her tone, no anger, only kindness, gentleness. Understanding he had sought his whole life and only found in Benedict.

"I cannot express the mess I'm in," he said.

Benedict moved forward now, and he stood on the other side of the desk and rested his hands on the surface. "Tell it, Darrius."

His breath exited his lungs in a long, shuddering sigh. The dam was going to break, it seemed. There was no stopping it.

"Debts, debts, all the debts," he said. "I do not think I've begun to find the half of them. There are women across London and half the countryside who have been misused by him. The servants in two estates are ready to revolt because of unpaid wages. And the word of his disgusting behavior with you, Vanessa, has spread, as well as the shocking details of his wagers on the carriage race he died in. Apparently, he also cheated in the race. He tried to run someone else off the road to win and *that* was what caused the accident."

Now that he'd said it all, he sank down in the chair and covered his face. "It will take me years to dig out of this disaster, if I ever can. So...so..." He struggled with what he had to say next. For their sakes. "You should be together away from this trouble. And leave me to it."

There was silence in the room for what felt like an eternity and then Benedict pushed at his hands, forcing him to lower them from his face. "No," he said, slowly and succinctly and with enough power that Darrius felt it in his bones.

"Fucking hell, Benedict," he grunted, and tried to get up, but Benedict pushed him back into the chair by the shoulders, even as he still loomed over the desk between them.

"No! I've given you far more than enough space in my life. I'm not abandoning you anymore."

"It's not abandonment," Darrius tried to argue.

"It is," Vanessa snapped. "And I will not leave you either. Look at me, Darrius."

He forced himself to do so and felt her light sink into him yet again. The light that he couldn't have for much longer.

"We won't be whole without each other," she said. Not whispered, not begged, said it, like it was so easy. Like she was so certain. And she was even more certain when she continued, "I love you, Darrius Warwick." She didn't let that stunning admission sink in before she added, "And I'm in love with him."

She motioned to Benedict, who smiled. He seemed less surprised by the admission than Darrius felt. "And I am also in love with you, you unbearable arse," Benedict said. "Even though you try very hard to make me stop. I love you with all my soul and heart. And I love her with everything in my being."

A tear slid down Vanessa's cheek and she wiped it away with a smile. Darrius felt the world tipping and he pushed to his feet, staggering away from them. "Don't do this. Not today. Not now when I can barely stay upright as it is."

Benedict came around the desk then and caught his lapels,

tugging him closer. "Then don't stay upright. Let *us* keep you upright."

Vanessa joined them and slid her arms around his waist, staring up at him. "Don't do this alone. You know you need us."

His knees felt weak as he stared at them, these two angels who had come into his life and made him believe, in the moments he had allowed it, that he could be happy. That he could have value beyond what he provided. That he could let go and never become what his family had become. That he could be loved and love with such a power that it took his breath away.

"I don't know," he whispered.

"Then let us do that for you, too," Benedict said before he leaned up and kissed Darrius.

It had been a lifetime since they'd kissed. Perhaps it was actually only a few days, but it felt like a lifetime. How had he gone so long before he allowed it? He didn't recall. In that moment, he just wanted to sink into him. While they kissed, Benedict reached for Vanessa and drew her to them. All three of their mouths moved together then, with heat and love and passion and support and everything in the world that mattered.

Darrius knew he couldn't refuse them. Not in this moment where he needed them to feel alive. Not after when they would wear his defenses down. So he surrendered. With a sigh, he broke away from them and walked across the room, feeling them track him, feeling their tension and worry.

When he locked the door, all that faded away. He turned back and leaned on the door. "Vanessa, you asked me not so long ago…or perhaps it was a lifetime ago, why I had denied myself my desire for Benedict all those years. Why I hardened myself to everything."

Her lips parted and she nodded. "Yes."

He shifted, trying to find the words he had always feared to say. Knowing they would hurt and heal in equal measure. "I suppose I told myself that it was another way to avoid being the scandal that the rest of my family was. But…but that wasn't why."

Benedict stepped toward him. "Then why?"

Darrius drank him in from his head to his toes, this man who he had loved for so long, he couldn't even remember when he had fallen. "Once I opened a door to you, Benedict, to wanting you, to loving you...I'd never be able to shut it. And it would endanger us both. Because...because Arthur knew about us. About my feelings for you. He held it over my head, even in his letter when he fled the country with Vanessa's maid."

Benedict was pale. "That was why you wouldn't show us the second page." Darrius nodded and then bent his head. Benedict's voice was hard when he said, "Why didn't you tell me?"

"Because I didn't want you to be harmed," Darrius whispered and glanced up at him. "I did it to protect you." He felt the tears stinging his eyes, especially when Benedict's expression softened, forgave. "I mourn my brother. And I also felt the surge of freedom that he could never harm me again, harm you. Harm her."

"Oh, my love," Vanessa said softly. "My two loves. I'm so sorry. Sorry for all the time you lost together. But please, Darrius, tell me that you won't give even more time away now. Please."

Darrius swallowed hard. This was the hardest thing he would ever do. And the best. And the brightest. "I need you both, so very much. Now. And if you can bear what will happen next...forever."

Vanessa made a soft sound of joy and Benedict seemed as though his knees buckled a little. But then they were moving toward each other, the kisses deeper and faster and harder and more driven. The troubles of the last few days faded, his grief faded, his worries about the future faded. They gave him that gift as Benedict shifted Vanessa between them so they could rock against her together.

Darrius stared down into her upturned face, so lovely and wonderful and somehow his. "I want us both to have you. Are you ready for that?"

She nodded. "I am. I can't wait."

"Good," he said and they backed toward the settee before the fire.

Benedict pushed him to sit and he did so, sprawling a little to create a place for Vanessa to settle herself. She did, pulling up her skirt to straddle his lap as she leaned down and kissed him with all the fire and warmth that he needed so desperately. He dug a hand into her hair, angling her mouth for better access and devouring her lips. God, he loved kissing her. Tasting her.

He opened his eyes and looked past her. Benedict was watching, but when their eyes met, he smiled. Darrius couldn't help but return the expression and it was the first time he'd done so since he'd received the news about his brother. But these two…they made him hope for a future.

He beckoned for him and Benedict moved forward. He pressed against Vanessa's back and she broke the kiss, leaning her head against Benedict's hip, her gaze unfocused as she cupped Darrius's cheek.

Benedict leaned in and tangled his fingers in hers. He kissed Darrius, deep and slow and Darrius moaned with the pleasure of it. "I love you," Benedict whispered against his lips, and Darrius drew back with a shuddering sigh.

Benedict moved to his knees behind Vanessa, lifting up into her, unfastening her as she went back to kissing Darrius. The heat between them rising, she began to grind against him with increasing little gasps and moans. His cock was rapidly hardening and he was lost. Lost in her, lost in them, lost in pleasure and love and hopes like he hadn't allowed himself in years, decades.

Her dress fell forward and Darrius tugged it down around her waist, along with her chemise. He bent his head and sucked her nipple, feeling the shivering reaction race through her body as Benedict chuckled, his lips against the back of her neck.

"Stand up," Darrius said. "Take the rest off. All of us need to take everything off right now."

She didn't hesitate. Benedict got to his feet and helped her as Darrius rose. He moved toward them, and together they all stripped each other, hands roving as they did so. When Darrius tugged his shirt over his head, Benedict stepped into him, kissing him as his hands glided along Darrius's ribcage. They groped lower and he unfastened the fall front of Darrius's trousers. When Benedict took his cock in hand and move over him in long, smooth strokes, Darrius's legs went weak.

"I love watching her with you," Benedict whispered. "I can't wait to feel you inside of her."

Darrius pulled back, staring into the dark eyes of this man he had loved and tried to distance himself from for so long. And now he never wanted to lose him. Never wanted to do anything but share his life.

"Let's not wait," he said, kissing him again before he stripped his trousers away. He returned to his seat on the settee and caught her hand. They returned to their original positions, only this time there was nothing separating their bodies. When she ground against him he felt the hint of her slick heat, saw the flush of her pleasure.

"I want you," she murmured as she shifted to align them. She kissed him as she took him into her body in a slow, steady slide. She gripped him and he lost his breath, watching her moan and writhe. She was his. Better yet, he was hers.

She settled herself fully on his lap and then looked back over her shoulder at Benedict. There was wickedness in her gaze, in her faint smile. "Hurry."

Benedict drew a small bottle from the pocket of his discarded jacket and returned to his position behind her. As Vanessa began to grind over Darrius, Benedict began to gently work at her arse, readying her for him. Darrius grunted as he felt the pressure of the other man's fingers through her sheath and shivered as he pictured how much more powerful it would be when it was Benedict's cock.

"He feels good, doesn't he?" he murmured, and Vanessa looked down at him, still wicked.

"So good, Darrius," she moaned. "You know how good."

He nodded and looked past her to Benedict. He was staring as he aligned his cock to her. Darrius stilled his own movements and helped to spread her a little wider as Benedict began to take her.

The stroke of him against Darrius's cock was so intense that he let out a soft cry in the quiet and bent his head to her shoulder. She was moaning and crying out, gripping his shoulders as her pussy flexed around him in mounting pleasure.

They stilled when Benedict was fully seated, leaning over them, his mouth on her shoulder, then seeking to meet Darrius when he shifted to kiss him. They were one, and it was magnificent.

Even more magnificent when the Darrius flexed up in her and felt Benedict thrust in return because neither of them could wait. They had to move. And it was better than Darrius ever could have imagined.

CHAPTER 13

Vanessa

Vanessa had pictured what it would be like to be taken by both men during their passionate time in the countryside. But nothing could have prepared her for reality. As in everything, they all moved together like they had been built to do so. Darrius and Benedict ground within her, pleasuring each other even as they lit her sensitive body on fire so powerfully that she feared she'd never come down.

She didn't want to come down. She just wanted to live like this, her body stretched, hands on her, mouths on her, both men moaning, her own voice cracking as she cried out while they thrust back and forth inside of her.

The pleasure was intense, powerful, never ending and building to a crescendo that felt more powerful than anything she'd ever felt before. Better yet, she saw and felt how much it meant to them, too. Darrius had released control and now his fingers dug into her hips, his cheeks flushed with pleasure. Behind her, Benedict grunted, swore, and his thrusts increased.

And when they both cried out, her body answered. They all

came together in a quivering mass of pleasure. She gripped them both through it, milking them to the end, her body rolling to the rhythm of pleasure and desire and love that was more powerful than anything else.

They lay together in a pile on the settee when it was over. Darrius's head rested on her breast, his thick hair tickling the sensitive flesh. She leaned back against Benedict's thighs. It was comfortable and quiet and she felt so at home. So loved. It almost didn't feel real.

"How will this work?" Darrius asked, breaking the silence.

She slid her fingers into his hair and combed there gently. "The same way it does with Merritt and Egerton and Peter. I've watched them together in their home since we returned to London. It isn't fraught or dangerous. It's life, Darrius." He lifted his head to look at her and she smiled at him. "We love each other. We support each other. We please each other, I hope every day. We *live*."

His expression softened a little and he sat up, cupping her cheeks to draw her in for a deep and powerful kiss that she felt in her blood and her bones and her heart. And when he drew back, he looked more open and ready then she'd ever seen him.

"I love you," he whispered. "I love you, Vanessa, so very much."

The joy that overtook her in that moment was complete and powerful and she couldn't help the tears that began to slide down her cheeks. She had begun that way with them, weeping over what hadn't happened. Now she wept for the delight of what could be, *would* be.

He kissed her again and then reached for Benedict. She held her breath. Their relationship had been harder. What he would say or do now would determine the rest of the path in a very different way.

Darrius

Darrius stared at Benedict. He had stared at him so many times over the years, but he really saw him now. Allowed himself to see and be seen. And not just Benedict's outrageous beauty, which haunted him day and night. But his intelligence, his wit, his kindness, his steadiness. His everything.

"And you," he said, his hands shaking. "My God, you." He touched his face. "You said earlier that I was an unbearable arse who tried to make you stop loving me. And you are right. I'm both those things. But you must know that I love you so deeply, Benedict. I'm painfully aware I've hurt you so deeply, as well. I do not know if I can ever make it up—"

"No," Benedict interrupted. "You hurt yourself. Not me."

Darrius leaned in and they kissed again. A promise this time. A vow, even though they'd not be allowed to take public vows. And though Darrius was completely and utterly happy in that moment, it did lead to a final question: "And what do we *do* now?"

Benedict nodded slowly. "I've been considering that. Vanessa, are you desperate to marry one of us over the other?"

She gasped. "Do not make me choose. I won't. I would marry you both right now and shock the city even more than they are already shocked."

"And you shall, privately," Benedict reassured her with a little smile for him. "But if you are not of a mind to decide, then I think you should be Darrius's wife."

"Mine?" Darrius gasped, and the vision that created was wonderful. Powerful. "I am not in disagreement, but I must ask you —why me?"

"Because a viscount needs a wife to be palatable," Benedict explained. "And if you marry Vanessa, you will be seen as what you are, a good man trying to make up for his brother's desperate mistakes."

Vanessa nodded. "He is right, my love. Especially when I make a fuss about just that. It will help you and me. Not to mention that I had a very nice dowry, which we will force my parents to pay if only so they do not look as terrible as they truly are."

Darrius blinked. "I do not want to marry you for money."

"Of course not. But why not have it?" Vanessa said with a laugh. "To pay the creditors and the wages and start to rebuild a very bad family name into one you...and I...and Benedict...can be very proud of?"

"But what about Benedict?" Darrius asked. "I have pushed him away for so long, I wouldn't do it again."

"You should know already," Benedict said, first kissing Vanessa and then kissing Darrius. "You couldn't lose me if you tried. I'm yours. Both of yours."

"Forever," Darrius said, completing the sentence and knowing it completed his life. They completed it.

And he had never been happier.

ALSO BY JESS MICHAELS

Theirs

Their Marchioness

Their Duchess

Their Countess

Their Bride

The Kent's Row Duchesses

No Dukes Allowed

Not Another Duke

Not the Duke You Marry

Regency Royals

To Protect a Princess

Earl's Choice

Princes are Wild

To Kiss a King

The Queen's Man

The Three Mrs

The Unexpected Wife

The Defiant Wife

The Duke's Wife

The Duke's By-Blows

The Love of a Libertine

The Heart of a Hellion

The Matter of a Marquess

The Redemption of a Rogue

The 1797 Club

The Daring Duke

Her Favorite Duke

The Broken Duke

The Silent Duke

The Duke of Nothing

The Undercover Duke

The Duke of Hearts

The Duke Who Lied

The Duke of Desire

The Last Duke

The Scandal Sheet

The Return of Lady Jane

Stealing the Duke

Lady No Says Yes

My Fair Viscount

Guarding the Countess

The House of Pleasure

Seasons

An Affair in Winter

A Spring Deception

One Summer of Surrender

Adored in Autumn

The Wicked Woodleys

Forbidden

Deceived

Tempted

Ruined

Seduced

Fascinated

To see a complete listing of Jess Michaels' titles, please visit:

http://www.authorjessmichaels.com/books

ABOUT THE AUTHOR

USA Today Bestselling author Jess Michaels likes geeky stuff, Cherry Vanilla Coke Zero, anything coconut, cheese and her dog, Elton. She is lucky enough to be married to her favorite person in the world and lives in Oregon settled between the ocean and the mountains.

When she's not trying out new flavors of Greek yogurt or rewatching Bob's Burgers over and over and over (she's a Tina), she writes historical romances with smoking hot characters and emotional stories. She has written for numerous publishers and is now fully indie.

Jess loves to hear from fans! So please feel free to contact her at Jess@AuthorJessMichaels.com.

Jess Michaels offers a free book to members of her newsletter, so sign up on her website:
http://www.AuthorJessMichaels.com/

facebook.com/JessMichaelsBks
instagram.com/JessMichaelsBks
bookbub.com/authors/jess-michaels